What Readers Are Saying about
Diamonds Dollars & Roses

"Wow!!! Love the book, especially the erotica parts."

"HOT!!"

"...your book was explosive and a page turner..."

"...amazingly written..."

"I visualized every kiss, lick, suck and moan."

"... made me laugh ..."

"You did an outstanding job on your book. Your time and investment has paid off..."

"This book has many twists that will keep you turning those pages to find out what happens next."

"I have read your book twice and I loved it. You do have a way with words and are very detailed in your character descriptions, emotions and setting the scene making you feel like you know exactly where they are."

"While reading the book, I couldn't wait to find out the significance of the book title. ...but decided to take the ride. I'm glad I did."

"I've read several romance novels written by women. But the romance in John's book is different, it's sweet yet erotic. As a trilogy, I can't wait to read what comes next!"

(continued on next page)

"I think what makes your book great is the raw thoughts and monologues, because come on we all have them. I think that is the best quality about your writing. Those raw thoughts and inner monologue make the characters human and relatable."

"Diamonds Dollars & Roses is an accurate tale of modern romance. It has all the craziness a new relationship can bring, and yet carries that real raw emotion of falling truly in love with someone while allowing yourself to be vulnerable."

"Bobby King and Brianna Woods are two young adults that are trying to make their way in this world and find their soul mate and in that, their life's plan together. As soon as you open the book Author J.A. Huguley words transport you into their world with his attention to detail, he makes you feel like you are a part of their story."

"This book has many twists that will keep you turning those pages to find out what happens next. Everything Bobby and Brianna go through are real life situations that many can relate to in one form or another. The way they get through each scenario is both surprising and heartwarming."

"It was exciting, with a rollercoaster of emotions and that's what I like in a book. I was up at Harborview looking for Bobby, praying he was ok."

"Bravo, Amazing John... well written, easy to read, and loved the story is in direct sequence with the title, 'Diamonds, Dollars and Roses'. You displayed oil and water of two people from different worlds both wanting LOVE. I loved Bobby's, patience in showing Brianna aggressive fire is not needed when two people love, trust, and respect each other. I can't wait for BOOK II."

"A straight up page turner"

Diamonds Dollars & Roses

ADULT URBAN FICTION

J. A. HUGULEY

www.johnhuguley.com

Print Rev. V
Update 11.13.XX
Published in the U.S.A.

Diamonds Dollars & Roses
Adult Urban Fiction

ISBN 978-0-578-77157-1

Consulting Editor: Nicole A. Calvo,
Author of the International selling book,
"The Ragdoll and The Marine"

Book Cover Design & Creation: John A. Huguley

Official Website: www.johnhuguley.com
Facebook: www.facebook.com/Author.John.A.Huguley
Instagram Photography: @john.a.huguley
Author Contact Information in the Back of the Book

Original Manuscript Written November 2018
First Print Version Released November 2020

Table of Contents

In memory of
Brian Lee Webster
…and all of the Holly Park Originals
that left us too soon. RIP

Foreword

In 2015, John A. Huguley I met through a chance encounter, which in hindsight has proven to be one of the most goal-achieving, and soul-satisfying relationships of my life. Although five years of friendship may not be a long time, the experiences we shared have brought about the creation of two literary works, numerous newspaper articles, and local & national publicity.

Mr. Huguley's propensity to encourage, nurture, and assist people to develop their God-given talent is what allowed me to write a memoir about my mother's experiences during World War II in the Pacific. He not only became my editor for the book but more importantly, served as a writing coach that spurred me on during some emotional and literary challenges of self-doubt and writer's block. His meticulous care in ensuring that my manuscript became published was just one of the many details that he took sole responsibility for. As a result, my book publication under his guidance and hard work, served as a stepping stone on his journey to complete — *Diamonds, Dollars & Roses.*

I was honored when John asked for my help as an assistant editor for this book, and having read *Diamonds, Dollars & Roses* several times, I realized that this man's talent was also his passion. It is often said to write what you know — this book takes place in a fictional world inspired by his life experiences. This urban literary work details the raw, gritty, and steeliness of the city streets and those who grow-up in it. The characters within these pages are of an underrepresented group of young adults — some of whom are tough on the outside yet innocent, while others are more mature and ambitious with a deep sense of family and resolve. Huguley takes the reader on a ride that moves through young love, street violence, urban struggles, family bonds, devotion, and heated passion. I found myself getting vested in the lives of those in this novel, and I am looking forward to discovering more about them. *Diamonds, Dollars & Roses* is the start of a trilogy of young urbanites whose struggle is real and heartfelt.

Nicole A. Calvo
Hagatna, Guam
Author of "The Ragdoll and the Marine"

Preface

In this crazy world we live in, sometimes we need to escape reality. My goal in writing this book is to take you away for a few hours and hopefully when you return you will be left wanting more.

In November 2018, I wrote this adventurous story filled with action, excitement and stimulating adult passion. After two-years of editing and fine tuning, I've produced a book that I'm proud of and I hope you enjoy!

It's not the destination, it's the journey.

~ John A. Huguley

WARNING: If you are offended by adult language, adult situations, or sexually explicit content, this is not the book for you. Please stop now and give the book to a friend or return it to me. This book is not for the morally judgmental or those with failing hearts.

Introduction

From the suburbs of Seattle to the streets of LA and back, hardworking Bobby King pursues the sexy and impulsive Brianna Woods thinking she is the love of his life - only to find out she's not into men. But after this dynamic pair from two different worlds are pulled together by a passion that neither can resist, they face unpredictable situations that try to rip them apart.

This book is full of diverse characters that you will either love or hate; violent ex-girlfriends, bad neighbors, call-girls, street thugs in prison - and an unhappy wife in a relationship so toxic, she'd rather kill her husband than allow him to go astray any longer. As you flip the pages, you will be kept on your toes, wondering what's coming around the next corner. Come dive into this action-filled adult urban fiction - served up with unexpected plot twists - and a side of erotica.

Ch. 1 - Love at First Flight

It's 2012, July 2nd, Monday afternoon. The Seattle-Tacoma International Airport corridors are full of anxious holiday travelers coming and going. Flight announcements are being broadcasted over the PA system every few minutes as people dodge and weave to avoid colliding into each other.

Among the hundreds of scattered vacationers scuffling through the airport is a 6-foot tall, chocolate-brown man in his late twenties. He is clean-cut, with dimples and strong facial definition. He's dressed relaxed for his upcoming flight — wearing jeans, sneakers, and his old college basketball hoody. He walks briskly while pulling his large travel suitcase behind him — occasionally glancing at strange faces that appear as lost as he is.

When he reaches Gate-29 where he'll be catching his departing flight, he stops in his tracks to double-check his ticket one last time.

His final travel destination is South Central LA, where he will spend the next two weeks with family. He will be picked-up at LAX Airport by his aunt and uncle whom he hasn't seen since he was a teenager. After graduating from college six-years ago, he landed a *suit-and-tie* sales job which has kept him grounded and away from traveling much.

He finds an open group of seats near his departing gate — this will be the perfect place to sit undisturbed in the airport waiting area until his flight arrives. To pass time, he sits and scrolls through social media on his phone while listening to an R&B music stream.

With just thirty-minutes left before his flight, he notices a beautiful cinnamon-brown-skinned woman in her mid-twenties — towing an old suitcase. She's petite but curvy, with two braids that run back from her temples to her shoulders.

She doesn't make eye contact while entering the same waiting area as him. She parks her luggage and sits in one of the vacant seats facing his direction.

He straightens up in his seat and thinks, *'Damn, she's FINE!'*

He takes advantage of her looking down at her phone to fully check her out.

She has lightly freckled cheeks that compliment her brown eyes. She's dressed casual but trendy — wearing a pair of large hoop earrings. On the left side of her neck is a four-inch wide tattoo that spells *Daisy*.

She notices his stares and glances up for a second — then rolls her eyes and looks back down to her phone.

But that is the signal he needs to confirm she saw him. Sitting only ten-feet from each other, he lifts his chin and in a deep voice introduces himself, "Hi — I'm Bobby!"

There's an awkward pause.

She sighs and gives another eye-roll before speaking, quietly she says, "…sup," then looks back down.

He continues talking, "I'm flying to LA to visit my aunt and uncle. I haven't seen them in fifteen-years."

There's another pause — still looking down, she doesn't bother responding this time.

He asks, "So, where are you flying to?"

In a soft but irritated tone she looks up, "Look bro, I like girls — I'm not into guys — don't waste your time."

Feeling shut down he snaps back, "I like girls too! — So now that we got that out the way, where are you flying to?"

She raises her voice, "Look bro…"

But before she can get another word out, he cuts her off, "I told you my name is Bobby — Please don't call me 'bro' again!"

She frowns and readjusts her posture.

He continues, "I'm simply waiting on a flight and I was trying to be a gentleman and speak!" He takes a deep breath and lowers his voice to a whisper, *"So lil Ms. Sassy — get your delicate little panties out of your ass and drop that funky attitude."* He slides forward in his seat, *"Now tell me, where are you flying to!"*

She curls her lips and looks him straight in the eyes, "My name ain't lil Ms. Sassy! It's Brianna!! Get that shit straight boy! — and I'm flying to the same place as you — DUMB-ASS! — Can't you see we're both waiting on the same damn flight? — Duhh!"

There's a long uninterrupted pause while they both stare each other down — waiting for the other to crack first. Just as Bobby is about to give up and go back to what he was doing before she walked up, she smirks and adds, "Besides, I'm not wearing any panties boy!"

Caught completely off guard, Bobby can't do anything but grin. Then they both start laughing. Neither had ever been so irritated, yet so amused by a stranger in such a short amount of time. There is some type of bizarre *yin-yang* connection between the two of them. With a coolness about himself, Bobby gets out of his seat and moves over to sit next to Brianna. She smiles and doesn't resist his advancements. They sit and have small talk for the next *twenty-five minutes* — until their plane arrives.

When it's time to board the plane the two of them walk side-by-side through the jet bridge. Brianna peeks up at Bobby while feeling an unexplained sense of security with this man she just met.

When they reach the door to the plane there is a gorgeous Ethiopian woman greeting the passengers. Brianna quickly glances at the attendant's name badge and politely asks, "Dani, is it possible to arrange for me and my brother to sit next to each other during the flight?"

The flight attendant smiles and kindly ask them to step to the side while she sees what she can do.

Bobby grins and whispers, *"So I'm your brother now?"*

They both laugh as other passengers are seated first.

Moments later Dani returns and guides the couple to an open set of seats in the back of the plane.

The 3-1/2-hour trip from Seattle to LA is full of friendly conversation and laughter. Bobby and Brianna talk as if they have known each other all their lives. They feel comfortable enough to hold hands through moments of heavy turbulence — and again during the landing in LA.

Stepping off the plane, Bobby thinks, *'Where will we go from here? Will this be the beginning of a new friendship, or will it end just like it started — in an airport?'*

As the two of them walk over to retrieve their luggage, they're both quiet. Then Bobby says, "Wait here – don't move!" as he quickly walks off. He returns with a yellow *Hertz rental car* brochure with his number written on the front and hands it to Brianna. He tells her to give him a call or text anytime she wants to chat or laugh again. Without saying a word, Brianna gives Bobby a tight hug and looks up into his eyes before slowly letting go and turning to walk away. He stands and watches her leave — pulling her old tan suitcase behind her.

For the first three nights after the flight, Bobby thinks about Brianna non-stop. But after not hearing from her, he begins to think about her less each day.

For the next two weeks, Bobby has a great time with his family in LA — his holiday vacation goes by fast. Now it's time to fly back home to

Seattle — back to the rat race of the corporate world.

***

After a long first week back at work in Seattle, Bobby gets a text message one afternoon from an unknown number. He raises his phone to read it.

All the text says is, *{I miss u!}*

Bobby racks his brain trying to figure out who it could be. Even though Bobby still thinks about Brianna, and she comes to mind as a possibility, he thinks there is no way she would text the words, *'I miss you.'*

After five-minutes of contemplating how to respond, Bobby sends back a simple yet cliché text, *{who dis?}*

Within seconds he gets a reply that reads, *{Stop playin boy! This is Brianna! U better not have no other females missing you! j/k lol}*

Bobby responds, *{You're the only one playing games girl! I get off work soon. Call me at 5:45 pm. SHARP!}*

{Yeah whatever! Don't tell me what to do boy!! lol}

With only two hours left in his workday, all he can do is think about Brianna and recall what she looked like the first time he laid eyes on her. Her beautiful brown skin, light freckles, coffee brown eyes and two thick braids. He remembers she was wearing a low-cut designer T-shirt with no bra, revealing her perky breasts. He also remembers she had a black leather bracelet embroidered with small rainbow-colored beads.

Although Brianna *said* she was into girls, Bobby is sure there is a sexual attraction between the two of them.

At 5:30 pm, Bobby leaves his office, jumps in his black Lexus sedan, and drives down the street to a city park that he likes to sit and chill on his lunch breaks. He leans the seat back in his car and waits for her call. At precisely 5:45 pm his phone rings.

He answers, "Sup girl?"

She responds in an excited voice, "Hi square, what are you doing?"

"Thinking about your beautiful smile!"

There is a long pause and neither one of them say anything. Bobby feels at this point there is nothing to lose. He wants to see where her mind is at. After the long uninterrupted silence, Brianna breaks rank and speaks next, "I'm back in Seattle — on Capitol Hill. Where do you live?"

"I live in a ghetto ass apartment complex out by the airport. It's a bit crazy, lots of loud music at night, and random people screaming in the hallways. Initially I was okay with it, but after a few years it takes a toll. On the bright side — rent is cheap, and it allows me to save money for bigger things. How about you?"

"I'm temporally living with two female roommates. One used to be my girlfriend until she cheated, and we broke up. It's an awkward living situation. To make things worse, Daisy and the other roommate are sneaking around sleeping with each other."

When Bobby hears the name *'Daisy'* he recalls the tattoo on the side of Brianna's neck as he sits quietly and listens to her talk.

She goes on to tell him how she wants to move but can't afford to rent an apartment by herself at the moment. The pair talk for hours just like the first time they met. After their long telephone conversation, they end the call just like they ended their first meeting, not knowing when they will see each other, or talk again.

Although he has her phone number now, he decides to leave it up to Brianna once again to make the next move.

Three more weeks will pass before they talk again.

Ch. 2 - Homeless

Six-weeks have gone by since Bobby and Brianna first met. Just like the first unexpected text, Brianna sends another message while Bobby's at work, *{I need your help! I need you to come n 'get me. Please!!!}*

The moment he reads the message he gets a lump in his throat. Concerned that she could be hurt he texts back immediately, *{Of course! Tell me where you're at!}*

She replies with the names of two cross streets at an intersection in downtown Seattle. She tells him that she can be there at 5:00 pm.

Bobby leaves work early to ensure that he will make it on time. He pulls up to the intersection about ten-minutes early and spots Brianna already there. She's sitting at a covered bus stop. On the bench next to her is a large tote bag. On the ground in front of her is the same old tan suitcase that she had when they first met. She looks different than she did at the airport. Now she looks sad and homeless. Overdressed for this warm summer weather. She's wearing a black bomber jacket with the hood pulled over her head. Baggy blue sweatpants with yellow 'UCLA' printed down the leg. She doesn't see Bobby in his car sitting at the light across the intersection.

When the traffic signal changes, Bobby drives up to the bus stop and jumps out of the car. He quickly walks around to open the door for Brianna. Then grabs her bags. He tells her to get in the car and relax. He opens the back door and lays her bags across the seat.

While in the car she doesn't say a word. She pulls her hood further over her head and slides her hands into her jacket pockets as if she's trying to disappear. Bobby lets her have her space while he drives around the city — with no particular destination. Without talking they cruise the Alki Beach strip with the sunroof open while listening to music playing in the background. As it begins to get dark Bobby drives up to a hilltop parking spot with a full view of the Seattle skyline. It's mid-August and the evening sky is incredibly clear. They can see for miles. They both sit in silence while taking in the view of city lights, neighborhood hills, and tops of skyscrapers.

After a few minutes of stillness Brianna speaks first, "Aren't you gonna ask me what happened?"

"Naw, you'll tell me if you want me to know."

She blurts out, "I got into a fist fight with those two bitches I live with!"

Without responding Bobby sits staring at the view.

She goes on, "They ganged up on me and told me I needed to move out," Brianna's eyes start to water as she continues, "but I have nowhere to go!"

Bobby predicts that she will ask for help finding a place to live, but before she does, he responds, "You can come stay with me."

She drops her head into her hands and cries quietly. After a few moments she lifts her head, "I don't deserve your help. I should have stayed in touch."

Bobby responds, "We were never apart! I thought of you every day and I know you did the same," he continues, "let's go grab some food and get you settled so you can get some rest."

She stares at the side of his face while he starts the car and drives off. During the ride, the two of them are completely comfortable with each other's silence.

After picking up Teriyaki-to-go at a spot around the corner from Bobby's place, they pull into a carport in front of 'Building D' at the *Sky-View* apartments. Bobby hands Brianna his house-key and the white plastic bag with their food in it. He opens the backdoor of his car and grabs her suitcase and tote. The two of them walk side-by-side toward the apartment building stairwell. Brianna feels a sense of déjà vu as if they have made this walk together in the past.

Bobby says, "It's unit #D201, on the second floor. Ignore the urine smell coming from under the staircase."

She chuckles, "Aww that's nothin, the hallway in my apartment building smells like sweaty ass holes!"

They both burst out laughing as they go up the stairs together. On the second floor Bobby's unit is the first one on the right. As Brianna sticks the key in and opens the door her face lights up with a smile. His apartment is cozy and smells fresh. There is a house plant in one corner, and a large comfortable couch in the middle of the room facing a wall mounted television.

"Make yourself at home," Bobby says, "the bathroom is down the hall on the left."

She kicks off her shoes at the door, "I do have to pee, I'll be right back!"

As she shuffles toward the restroom she passes Bobby's bedroom on the opposite side of the hallway. She quickly takes a peek before stepping into the bathroom.

He has a king-size bed with no headboard, a dark wood dresser, and two nightstands. The room is clean, and his bed is made. No television that she can see.

While she's in the bathroom, Bobby sets up the food at a small dinner table next to the kitchen. Just as he finishes tossing the styrofoam boxes in the trash, she steps into the dining area and says, "I guess I don't have to worry about you making a move on me!" while giggling, "because only gay guys keep their apartments as clean as you do!"

Unamused, he replies, "I'm glad you think that's funny — now sit your smart ass down and let's eat before the food gets cold."

As they eat, Brianna dominates the conversation talking about her recent roommate situation. Then she suddenly stops speaking and says, "What are you staring at?"

"Your brown eyes," he says.

"I told you I'm into girls. I'm a lesbian. Now stop it, you're making me feel uncomfortable."

Bobby sarcastically responds, "Yeah whatever. And like I told you, I also like girls — so that must mean I'm a lesbian too!"

She rolls her eyes, "That shit's not funny!"

They finish their food without talking anymore. Then Bobby gets up from the table, flips on the TV, and sits on the couch. Brianna stays in the kitchen rinsing the plates and placing them in his dishwasher before joining him.

He asks, "So what do you like to watch?"

"I don't watch a lot of television. I mostly read books in my downtime."

He thinks to himself, *'A book reader — that's a sexy quality in a woman!'*

Brianna finishes in the kitchen and walks over to the couch to stretch out next to Bobby. Without asking she lays down and rests her head on his lap. After a few minutes — the feeling of her head on his thigh combined with his strong attraction for her causes him to get erect. She notices and quickly lifts up, "Are you serious? Are you getting a boner!?"

Embarrassed, Bobby pauses before answering, "Sorry — I can't help it."

She slowly rolls her eyes and lays her head back down on his lap. She grins to herself, and quietly mumbles, *"Well calm down boy!"*

Bobby ignores her comment. He is relaxed after the meal and closes his eyes while he caresses her shoulder. Although he doesn't make any moves, he imagines kissing her neck and cheeks. Brianna also closes her eyes, and for the first time that she can recall, a man is sexually arousing her — it feels natural and she wants to be closer to him.

For the next hour they don't say a word, nor do they move as their internal passion for each other grows. Then without warning she nervously looks up at Bobby and whispers, *"Let's go lay down on your bed!"*

Ch. 3 - Pillow Talk

Fully clothed, the pair lay on top of his bed in silence — holding hands and listening to the loud music and other sounds coming from outside the apartment.

After thirty-minutes Bobby turns and whispers, *"I'm sorry for what you're going through. I'll help in any way I can."*

She sniffles, "Thank you!" then starts to cry while she snuggles into his arms. Once she catches her breath, she asks for some tissues.

"I have something softer for you," he reaches in his nightstand drawer and pulls out a fresh white cotton t-shirt, "here, use this!"

Without hesitation, Brianna takes the shirt and wipes her tears, then she blows her nose. They both start laughing. Brianna scoots up in the bed and kisses Bobby on his cheek before nesting herself in his arms again.

For the next two-hours Brianna reveals more about her life story.

Her family and friends call her Bri for short. Brianna was raised by a single mother. Brianna's mom, Nina, is a first generation Mexican-American, born and raised in East LA.

Brianna never met her biological father and her mom never mentions him, other than the fact that he was African-American. Brianna believes that her mother would have never revealed that her father was Black except Bri has predominantly Black physical features which couldn't be hidden or ignored growing up.

Brianna has a fifteen-year-old half-brother named Junior who still lives at home. His father is

Chicano and lives in Oakland — a five-hour drive away.

Brianna dropped out of high school her sophomore year and moved in with a teenage girlfriend that she grew up with. Her girlfriend Mia moved out on her own at age sixteen to get away from an abusive household. Brianna and her girlfriend lived as roommates for two-years before Bri got tired of the apartment being a revolving door for Mia's ever-changing rotation of thuggish boyfriends.

One Friday night while attending a block-party concert in South Central LA, Brianna met a Samoan girl named Daisy who she hit it off with. Daisy is five-foot-eleven and has a body of an Olympic volleyball player. Daisy is a few years older than Bri — at the concert she was wearing booty shorts and a tank top with no bra. It was Daisy's body confidence that first caught Bri's attention.

The two have similar personalities and interests. After the concert, they started hanging out regularly by going to clubs and other shows together. Being older and more experienced, Daisy had a large influence on Brianna. When going out, Daisy was always "dressed to impress" — which had a lot to do with the way Bri dresses now.

While the two ladies were getting to know each other, Bri expressed her frustration with her living situation with Mia. Daisy offered to let her move in to her two-bedroom apartment — Bri accepted without hesitation.

Being a roommate with her new friend was a lot different than living with Mia. There were no guys coming and going. The two of them spent many evenings at home just chilling, talking, or watching movies.

The bond between them grew stronger over time and eventually turned into Bri's first romantic relationship. Although Bri didn't feel that Daisy was her soul mate, she later took a chance in the relationship by moving to Seattle with Daisy for what she believed would be a positive change of environment.

While sharing her life stories Brianna starts getting sleepy, "Bobby, am I talking too much?'

"Naw – not at all — I appreciate you for sharing," then he kisses her on the cheek.

The longer she talks she starts to slur from exhaustion and eventually passes out in his arms. After Brianna falls asleep Bobby lays in the dark room staring at the ceiling while reflecting on what she just told him about her life growing up in Los Angeles.

Although it's a lot for Bobby to absorb in one night, he's happy to know more about the woman that he admires so much. Still on top of the covers and fully clothed, it's now past 1:00 am and he now drifts off to sleep.

A few hours pass — Bobby wakes first and is instantly aroused by the warmth of Bri's body next to him and her womanly scent. Without considering the consequences he takes a deep breath to inhale her essence, triggering his mind to spin with sexual thoughts and desires. He lays there until he can't stay silent any longer.

He whispers, *"Bri — psst... wake up — wake up Bri!"* Lightly rocking her body, repeating, *"babe... babe... psst... wake up..."*

She slowly opens her eyes. Barely awake she looks at Bobby and immediately climbs on top of him. Still in her drawstring sweatpants, she begins to grind on Bobby's thigh while passionately kissing him.

He can't believe what's happening! As much as he wants her, he is not willing to have a one-night stand that may turn awkward later. He only intended to wake her up to talk more and get his mind off his sexual thoughts.

Laying under her, he wraps both arms around Brianna's waist and hugs her tightly until her grind comes to a halt.

He pulls his mouth away from her hot kisses and whispers, *"Hold on — I don't want you to do anything you'll regret!"*

Bashfully she pulls away from Bobby's grip. She slides out of bed and dashes to the restroom across the hallway. Before closing the bathroom door behind her, she says, "I'm sorry, I'm so embarrassed!"

He stays in the bed wondering if he should go knock on the bathroom door to see if she's okay, or just give her space. After a minute of silence Bobby gets out of bed and stands in the dark hallway and talks through the door, "You have nothing to be sorry for! — I was the one that woke you up because I was horny — I'm the one that is embarrassed — that was selfish of me! — Please come back in the bedroom!"

There's no response from Brianna.

Then Bobby hears the shower come on and sees a ray of light coming from the door opening, *"Come in here!"* she says.

Bobby slowly pushes open the door just in time to see Brianna step into the shower.

"Come get in with me!"

Bobby is almost breathless with disbelief as he takes off his clothes and steps in behind her.

She's facing the shower head, so all he can see is her back side. As her two braids get wet, she asks Bobby to take her hair down. He reaches up and starts unbraiding her hair from the back. He pulls his fingers through her long hair as the hot water causes it to curl up into a relaxed afro.

When he's finished taking down her hair, she thanks Bobby by turning around to face him — revealing what he has only imagined until now. Her dark brown nipples are aroused from the stimulating hot water drizzling over her chest. Her pubic hair is short, curly, and glittering with beads of water.

Bobby looks deep into her coffee brown eyes — gazing into her soul. He feels a lump in his throat as his heart pounds with a passion beyond anything he's ever felt. Most men would want to take this beautiful woman right there. But Bobby only wants to hold her in his arms and enjoy the moment. Brianna can see the genuineness in his eyes as if she can read his mind.

She wraps her arms around his waist, laying her head against his chest. Under the shower stream they stand there feeling each other's heartbeats until the water starts to run cold.

Giggles erupt from them both as they hurry to rinse off and step out of the chilly shower.

As Brianna bends over to towel off her legs — he can't help staring, "You have a gorgeous body."

She turns back and whispers, *"Thanks,"* then bashfully looks away.

The two of them finish drying off and climb back into the bed — under the covers and nude this time. Controlling their sexual desires, they snuggle back to sleep until it's time for Bobby to get ready for work.

While getting dressed to leave, Bobby reaches in a drawer and hands Brianna an extra key to his apartment, "Here, I want you to make yourself at home — *mi casa es su casa.*"

Brianna blushes, "I'm going to make it up to you, I promise! Today I'll be out looking for a new job."

Not only was Brianna living with Daisy, she also works at a large book store that Daisy manages — so she never wants to return to that job ever again. He understands and asks if she needs any help with money.

"Thanks Bobby, but no thanks! — I have a few dollars in savings. Plus, I want to pay you back for everything you're doing for me."

"I don't need you to pay me anything — I don't want anything but truth from you."

Like a giddy little girl, she prances over to Bobby, stands on her tip toes, and gives him a kiss on the lips. "You are a special man!"

Bobby smiles and walks out the door to work.

Ch. 4 - The Phone Call

Three weeks have gone by since Brianna moved in with Bobby. She has a new job as a server at a pancake house near the airport on Pacific Highway.

The relationship between her and Bobby is full of flirtation and sensual teasing. Although they haven't had sex, intimate kissing and cuddling during the night is a regular occurrence. Both are waiting for the other to step-it-up and propose that it's time to take things to the next level — and make it official.

Brianna's work shift ends earlier than Bobby which allows her to get home first. She's having fun preparing dinner each evening, so food is ready when Bobby walks in.

Tonight, Brianna spends extra time on a nice meal and finds a single candle to place on the small dining area table.

When Bobby comes home from work and opens the door, he immediately smells the savory aroma of the meal she just put her heart and soul into. Brianna runs over and kneels to unlace Bobby's shoes, then takes his hand and guides him to the table. As he sits down, Bobby cannot control his cheek-to-cheek grin.

"What's the special occasion?" Bobby asks.

"Us babe!" She smiles while placing two plates of shrimp fettuccine on the table. As Brianna turns to walk back in the kitchen for the drinks, Bobby's phone rings.

He hits speakerphone and answers without checking who it is, "Hello!"

A female voice says, *"Hi Honey! – How are you doing?"*

"I'm doing good! I'm about to eat dinner though — can I call you back later?"

"Sure – just call me tomorrow, I'm going to bed early tonight. I just wanted to say hi!"

As Bobby hangs up Brianna sits down at the table not saying a word. Her face changes from happy to sad during that fifteen-second call.

"What's wrong Bri?"

"Nothing," Brianna replies quietly while looking down at her plate and twirling her fork in the noodles.

There is a long silent pause — then Brianna stands up and explodes, "WHO THE FUCK IS THAT?!"

Bobby leans back as if he's just seen a demon appear before his eyes.

"WHO THE FUCK IS THAT BITCH THAT JUST CALLED YOU HONEY?!"

Without losing his cool, Bobby calmly replies, "A friend — but seriously, I don't owe you an explanation why someone that I've known for years calls me — besides, you're not even my woman..." Bobby tightens his eyes and stares straight into Brianna's face, "...and don't ever cuss at me like that again!"

Realizing that she is in the wrong for reacting like she did, Brianna sits down at the table and doesn't say a word.

"Thank you!" Bobby says, "now let's eat and talk about it later — this food looks delicious!"

Feeling embarrassed, she agrees to drop it for now but slips in little apologies throughout the meal.

The food is prepared to perfection — they both eat every bite. Bobby does not want the entire evening ruined after Brianna's outburst, so he cracks a few jokes at the table to lighten the mood.

After dinner, Bobby gets up and walks over to the couch to sit down.

"Bobby, can I come join you after I clean up the kitchen?"

"Babe — of course you can — you don't have to ask that."

She thinks to herself, *'oh my god, he still called me 'babe' even after that bullshit display I just put on!'* She begins to tear up while putting the plates in the dishwasher.

After cleaning the kitchen, Bri wipes her eyes and enters the living room with Bobby. They sit on the couch and talk. She apologizes again for exploding at the table. Bobby is transparent and says he's not that upset about it. In fact, he was a bit flattered.

"Bobby, can I ask you a few questions about that female on the phone?"

"Yeah sure — what do you want to know?"

"Have you ever had sex with her?"

"I have — but it was several years ago, and now we're just friends."

"Have you ever had sex with her in the same bed that we've been sleeping in?"

Bobby pauses for a second before answering, "Yeah — I have."

Brianna frowns for a second — then does her best to put on a straight face before continuing, "Sorry, I can't help myself. When I care about someone I can get really jealous. It's a bad quality I know. I wish I could control it."

"It's okay Bri — just try not to explode like that again. If you have questions you can ask me, and we can talk it out calmly like we are now."

"Thanks, I appreciate you!" she sniffles. Still upset she continues, "but I really don't want to get back in the same bed that you had sex with another woman in — I'll sleep on the couch from now on."

"Okay — I understand," Bobby takes a deep breath and gets up from the couch. He walks down the hallway and opens the linen closet to grab a fresh set of sheets and blankets. Brianna stays on the couch until he returns.

He walks back into the living room with a grin, "Well you're gonna have to get up so I can make the bed."

Caught off guard by Bobby's nonchalant actions, Brianna stands up and steps to the side. She watches him tuck the sheets into the couch cushions and wonders why he's so quick to agree to her request and doesn't try to change her mind. But as she gets to know him better she's recognizing that he is level headed and wouldn't do anything spiteful or to intentionally hurt her. So, she goes with the flow to see what comes next.

He finishes and asks, "So front or back?" while pointing at the new makeshift bed.

Brianna suddenly realizes Bobby is going to sleep on the couch with her. She smiles hard, and with an innocent blush answers, "Front of course!"

They both laugh and snuggle in for the night. It's been a long day, and after the emotional outburst over the phone call, Brianna starts drifting off to sleep. The two of them are like one as they lay close together. The back of her neck against his lips, his arms wrapped around her waist, and her butt pressed against his body. She loves being so close to him and cherishes knowing that she turns him on. She has never felt so safe — or so wanted in all her life.

She bashfully whispers, *"Bobby, I want to be your woman."*

He kisses her on the back of her neck and whispers, *"Babe, you're already my woman — and you have been since the first time I laid eyes on you — I've just been waiting on you to figure this out."*

She turns and kisses him on the lips, *"I will be the best woman to you ever — I promise!"*

Bobby's heart pounds at the sound of her words, *"We are going to be the best to each other!"*

They both close their eyes and fall asleep.

Ch. 5 - Surprise & Fortunes

It's Friday morning — Brianna gets up and leaves to work first. Within minutes of walking out the door, she sends Bobby a text message apologizing for being jealous and selfish about the bed. She tells him there's no need for them to sleep on the couch another night.

***

After work, Brianna arrives back at the apartment where she witnesses two huge men in blue coveralls carrying Bobby's old mattress down the building staircase. She stands and watches them load the bed into a large white moving truck before they drive off.

The front door to the apartment is wide open. She walks in, quickly takes off her shoes and rushes to the bedroom. She can't believe her eyes as she stops and stares at a giant dark wood bed built for a king. There are four enormous bedposts that reach to the ceiling — with a headboard the size of a china cabinet. The bottom of the bed is a foot off the floor — while the top of the mattress is as high as her waist. She has never seen a bed so big in her life.

While taking it all in, Bobby silently walks up behind her, "Surprise! Now you will be the only woman to ever sleep in *this* bed!"

She turns and jumps into Bobby's arms, "There is no one like you in this world!!" She plants a big kiss on him before spinning back around and jumping up onto the bed, "Come up here babe!"

He smiles, "Not yet, let's put sheets on it first," and points to a new Egyptian Cotton bedding set sitting on the dresser.

"Oh my god, you got new sheets too!" she blushes, "Tonight — I'm going to give you something *extra* special!"

The couple make their new bed together, then go out for dinner. Bobby takes Bri to a traditional Chinese food restaurant on the other side of town that he grew up eating at. On the drive Brianna is on cloud-nine, and thinks to herself, *'this day couldn't get any better.'*

Upon arriving at the restaurant, a little old woman wearing a red silk jacket embroidered with gold dragons greets the couple. She seats them in a comfortable booth surrounded by traditional Chinese décor.

Before the woman walks away Bobby says, "We know what we want if you'd like to take our order now."

"Yes sir, what would you like?"

"May we have an order of — shrimp fried rice, vegetable chow mien, egg-fu-young, lemon fried chicken wings, and sweet n' sour prawns with the sauce on the side?"

Brianna smiles and whispers, *"Yum, that all sounds delicious!"*

The lady asks, "Would either of you like anything to drink?"

Brianna blushes, "May I have a Shirley Temple with a few extra maraschino cherries?"

"Yes dear — and for you sir?"

"Just tea for me," before adding, "oh, and may I have a side of hot mustard?"

The woman politely bows before turning and walking towards the kitchen double doors to put in their order.

"Babe — you ordered a *lot* of food."

Bobby laughs, "I always order the same entrees. It will be plenty to eat here with enough left to take home."

Brianna smiles, "I'm definitely not complaining babe, this is your spot! Besides, everything you ordered sounds good to me! I like this place already — thanks for bringing me here!"

The woman returns with the beverages.

While sipping her drink and giggling, Brianna can't stop fidgeting in her seat, "Just wait till I get you back to the apartment babe!" She suddenly stops squirming and stares into his eyes before softly saying, *"I love you!"*

Without hesitation Bobby responds, "I love you too!"

When the food arrives Bri can't believe how much food there is. They both dig in while exchanging flirty glances.

Near the end of the meal, the little old woman approaches the table with a warm smile. She bows and asks if there is anything else the couple would like. They both say no as the woman places the check on the edge of the table, along with two fortune cookies. She bows again, then turns and walks back towards the kitchen double doors.

Bobby opens his cookie first and reads his fortune to himself. He smiles and slides it across the table to Brianna.

She reads it out loud, *"A Large Sum of Money Is Coming Your Way."*

Bobby says, "Now that's what I'm talking about!"

They both laugh.

Next, Brianna cracks open her cookie and reads her fortune in silence. Her eyes turn red as she holds back tears. She stares at the little white piece of paper while Bobby waits patiently.

"Babe, what does it say?"

Brianna looks up and sniffles, "It says, *'Your New Life Begins Today.'"*

Bobby gets up from his seat and slides into Brianna's side of the booth. He places his arm around her shoulder and kisses her on the cheek.

A few minutes later the little old woman returns again with a stack of white Chinese food to-go boxes. The couple look at her and smile.

As the old lady boxes the extra food, she peeks up at the two of them sitting side by side. — With a thick accent, and wisdom in her voice she says, *"Together, the two of you are a powerful force. Apart, you are only half as strong as your full self. Never leave each other's side."*

***

Back at the apartment Brianna says she wants to take a hot bubble bath to be extra fresh for the new bed. In the back of Bobby's mind, he's sure this is the night they will consummate their relationship. They've spent every day and night together ever since Bri moved in. They have talked about everything from family, to religion, their childhoods, and even death. Bobby is sure that he wants to be with Brianna exclusively — and he's ready.

Brianna lays in the tub imagining what will happen soon while looking back at her life. During their late-night talks, she revealed to Bobby that she has not had sex with any guy since her first encounter as a teen. She was 15-years-old and didn't even like the boy she slept with. She only had sex to say she was no longer a virgin. Her second sexual encounter was at 17 — it was with a girl that was three years older than her.

Today Brianna realizes that she was seduced by the older girl at the time — but that girl made Brianna feel so good she couldn't resist. Even as an adolescent she always enjoyed looking at other girl's bodies. So, when that older girl made sexual advances on Brianna, it felt good, so she didn't resist it.

Brianna never went through the typical 'coming out' phase that many lesbians do. She was always open and comfortable with her sexual attraction to girls, and never hid it. Then came Bobby, and everything changed.

When she thinks of Bobby, she doesn't think of sexual identity in the sense that most people do — straight or gay. She sees him as her soulmate. He could have come to her in the body of a man, or a woman, and she feels she would have fallen for him just the same.

Every day that passes, Brianna falls deeper in love with Bobby even though they have not had intercourse yet. She thinks to herself, *'This must be true love.'*

After her long hot bubble-bath she steps out of the tub and takes a long look at herself in the mirror. She is starting to see a different woman emerge withing herself, and she loves what she's seeing.

She comes out of the bathroom smiling and wearing a white terrycloth robe with her hair wrapped in a towel. She asks Bobby if he minds if she has a glass of wine to relax. Bobby has an unopened bottle of red Pinot Noir on his kitchen counter that he saves for guests, "Sure babe, I'll pour you a glass."

Brianna snuggles into the couch with her glass of wine, while waiting on Bobby to take his shower.

When he finishes his shower, he steps out with just a towel tied around his waist. He stands at the edge of the living room, "How are you doing babe?"

She blushes while staring at the bulge in his towel, "I'm perfect *now*!"

They both smile at each other as he takes her by the hand and leads the way to the bedroom. Because the bed is so high Bobby helps her up on to it. She takes off her robe, lets down her hair, and sits up eagerly waiting for him to get on the bed with her. But he keeps his feet planted on the floor while laying her down.

The moonlight streams through the window blinds, casting stripes across Brianna's entire body as she lays on her back.

He places light kisses on the tops of her thighs, slowly working his way to her hips, and up the middle of her stomach. He strategically stays away from her womanly treasure. He slowly climbs up into the bed and continues to kiss her body while she lays back enjoying every bit of his love making. She trusts that Bobby knows what he's doing, so she patiently follows his lead. She is completely wet with anticipation. She wants it all. She needs to feel him inside her.

She whispers, *"Babe, please put it in me — I need to feel you now — please."*

"Okay — let me get a condom — hold on a sec."

"No! — Not the first-time babe! — The first time I want to feel all of you."

Bobby lifts up and looks deep into Brianna's eyes, "I want to feel *you* too!"

While holding his shaft in one hand, he lightly rubs the edges of her wet oasis with slow, caressing motions. When she can feel him starting to enter, she grabs his waist, arches her back, and draws him in. She can't believe what she is feeling. Her body is experiencing sensations she never knew existed.

Bobby takes his time — not entering all the way. He wants her to be completely comfortable. He wants this moment to be memorable.

Bobby looks into her eyes, *"I love you Bri,"* then slowly inhales her breath as she gasps with pleasure.

She can't hold back her tears of affection, *"I love you Bobby..."*

The two of them gaze into each other's souls while being perfectly connected below the waist. Neither wanting to rush the moment. Her body completely relaxes to allow him deeper into her body. He lightly kisses her cheeks and neck while tears run back along the sides of her face. Brianna feels so much love at this moment, that she thinks to herself — *if she died tonight, she would die a happy woman.*

Their love-making is spiritual — nothing kinky. Their two bodies woven together as one. There is no sense of time or space as the quiet evening passes. They are the only two people that matter in the world right now. Both exchanging kisses wherever they can reach without pulling apart.

As they continue to stare into each other's eyes, Bobby's pupils begin to dilate as he quietly snarls. At that moment she can feel his shaft growing larger inside of her. She thought she had him all the way in, but now she can feel him going in deeper. His face changes — his eyes tighten, and he shows his teeth.

A slight fear comes over Brianna as her heart begins to pound, not knowing what is about to happen next. His shaft is now fully erect as he pulls up on his knuckles like a gorilla. He gets up on his knees and starts thrusting inside of her body. She raises her knees to her chest so she can take all he has to give. She is so wet that she can feel her hot juices dripping down her ass as his scrotum slaps against her behind.

Her eyes roll back as she takes every stroke of his body. He is like a primal, jungle animal as he grunts while pushing deep inside of her. The light pain Brianna feels is pleasurable. She wants him to gently hurt her. She wants him to make her scream with ecstasy. She locks her stare on Bobby's eyes. Almost breathless she pushes out, "Oh Fuck — I can feel you so deep inside of me!"

His face tightens up as he arches his back and brings his mouth down to her ear — he quietly growls, *"Fuck — I'm about to cum babe!"*

At the sound of his voice to her ear, she can feel her orgasm ready to release. She curls her toes, grits her teeth, and screams with pleasure as she cums hard. The heat from her hot juices causes

Bobby to explode seconds later. He releases every ounce until it starts oozing back out onto the bed.

The two of them clench each other tight and lay there in silence — until they fall asleep in each other's arms.

Ch. 6 - Breakfast Can Wait

Saturday, the morning after the couple's first divine encounter is full of bliss and affection. Bobby has the confidence of superman, but he also knows he won't be able to live the rest of his life without Brianna in it. Brianna is experiencing an elevated level of happiness like nothing she's felt before. The two have bonded in a way that nothing can pull them apart.

"Bobby, have you ever thought about having kids?" Brianna asks while reaching in the refrigerator for eggs to make breakfast.

"I have — but never seriously I guess. What about you babe?"

While continuing to gather stuff to prepare the food she says, "I've always been with girls, so I never gave it much thought I guess."

Bobby walks up behind Brianna and places his hands on her hips, "I will give you a baby if that's what you're asking."

Brianna quickly reaches across the stovetop and turns off the burner, then runs into the bathroom and closes the door.

Bobby follows and stands in the hallway, "Babe, are you okay?"

She sniffles, "Yeah — I'm okay — I'll be out in a minute!"

A few minutes pass before she steps back out with red, puffy eyes and a ball of tissues in her hand.

"Bri, what's wrong?"

"You came inside of me last night. What if I'm pregnant?"

He wraps his arms around her waist, "I got you babe! – It's me and you from here on out!"

She hugs him tight, "You are too good to be true Bobby – please don't hurt me — please!"

He wraps his arms around her, "I fell in love with you the second you walked into my life – I never want to hurt you."

After letting out a sigh of relief she slowly pulls back, looks him in the eyes and bashfully giggles, "Well if I don't feed you breakfast soon your stomach is not going to love me."

Bobby takes her by the hand and whispers, *"Breakfast can wait,"* and leads her to the bedroom.

Just like their first union he lifts her onto the bed and lays her back. As he kisses the inner side of her knee he whispers, *"Babe — can I taste you?"*

"Oh Bobby — yes babe — yes…"

He takes his time and slowly moves her legs apart while lightly kissing up her inner thigh.

She grabs the closest pillow she can reach — and clenches it in her arms, "Fuck!! You're giving me chills!"

He makes sure that she's enjoying everything he's doing by listening closely to her moans and groans. He finds her sweet spot which triggers her greatest arousal and he stays there. As she grinds her hips in his face, he pauses just long enough to *whisper*, *"mmm... you taste so good,"* then continues.

She curls her toes and arches her back as she reaches her climax. Bobby can sense what is about to happen. He holds his position while hardly breathing.

Brianna starts to cry out with pleasure as she can't take it any longer, "Fuck! I'm about to cum! Stop! Please stop babe! — I'm about to cum hard!! — Please baby, put it in me — please — now!"

With his face covered in her juices, he lifts his head and smiles, "Alright babe — let me wipe my mouth."

Almost breathless she demands, "No! — bring your *handsome face* here and kiss me now!!"

Bobby does what he's told and climbs up over her. Looking down into her sparkling brown eyes he says, "I love you Bri!"

"I love you too Bobby!"

She pulls his face close and kisses the juices from his lips as he slowly inserts his shaft into her sacred fruit. The feeling of him going deeper into her body causes her orgasm to release immediately. She cries out, "I'm cumming! — I'm cumming!"

The sound of her sweet voice boosts his arousal. The warmth from her flowing nectar takes him to the edge. He can't hold back much longer. His eyes roll back as he thrusts deeper into her body. Brianna can tell Bobby is about to cum inside of her, but she doesn't want that to happen — she has a different plan.

She uses all of her strength to push him off, "Don't cum yet! — I want to taste you too!"

He can't believe his ears at first. With all her strength she pushes against his chest until he is laying on his back.

While holding his hard shaft in one hand, she softly kisses the tip and bashfully giggles, *"Please don't laugh, I've never done this before."*

Bobby lets out a deep breath, "Babe! — you don't have to do this if you don't want to."

"There's nothing else I'd rather do," she continues to give light kisses to his manhood. Then she places her warm mouth around the end of his rod while moving her head back-and-forth.

Bobby lays on his back enjoying every sensation while lightly running his fingers through her hair. The longer she pleasures him, the more intense his arousal becomes. He stretches both hands out to his sides and clenches the sheets in his fists. He cannot hold back, "Babe! – I can't take it any longer — I'm gonna cum!"

Hearing Bobby's growls of pleasure gets her extremely excited. She makes sure not to change her position. Then like a shaken soda bottle, he erupts in her hot mouth. She doesn't pull away until she takes it all.

His fists slowly open as his body goes limp, "Damn babe — you drained the life out of me."

While savoring his taste in her mouth, she reaches between her legs and starts to rub herself. Her deep love for him and their erotic engagement brings her to a second climax within seconds.

Out of breath and feeling fully pleasured — she rests her head on his thigh for a few moments. She whispers, *"I love you babe!"* before climbing under Bobby's arms and pulling the covers over the two of them. They kiss soft and slow for a few moments, then drift back to sleep.

An hour passes before Bobby opens his eyes first, looks around the room then wakes Bri with a kiss on her forehead. "Baby, let's eat something — I'm starving!"

Brianna smiles and kisses him back. She gets up and puts on her robe, "I'll go finish the breakfast I started this morning," and giggles.

While she is in the kitchen, Bobby walks in the bathroom to take a shower. By the time he's done the food is ready. They eat, and like a tag team she goes in and showers while he cleans the kitchen.

When Bri comes out of the bathroom she notices Bobby removing clothes from his dresser. He turns and looks at her, "These three drawers are all yours! – this is your home now."

She turns and picks up her wallet and pulls out her uncashed paycheck. She endorses the back and signs it over to Bobby. "I want you to take this and don't say no! I need to do this, so I feel right inside."

"Baby, you don't have to do that."

"Yes, I do. Please let me do this — I gotta know that I'm contributing to *our* home."

Bobby takes her check and sets it on top of the dresser next to his wallet.

Ch. 7 - Uninvited Guest

A few months have gone by and things are going great in the relationship. Today Brianna has the day off from work and is at home waiting for Bobby when there's a light knock on the apartment door. She quietly walks over and tiptoes to look out the peephole. She sees the top of a woman's head with long black hair looking down. Suddenly she hears keys jiggling as the knob starts to turn.

Fear of not knowing who could be entering Bobby's apartment, Brianna quickly backs up and runs into the bedroom. Having experienced a break in as a kid, Brianna's first instinct is to quickly climb under the bed. From her hiding spot she can hear the woman taking off her shoes at the front door and softly walking around the apartment as if she's inspecting things. As the woman enters the bedroom only her feet are visible from under the bed. Pretty brown toes that are well pedicured with bright red polish.

The woman slowly walks from one side of the bed to the other and mumbles with irritation in her voice, *"He must have a new bitch — he's got a new bed!"*

Bri's heart begins to beat faster as the woman stands in one place breathing hard. Then she hears the woman unzip — just before dropping her black skirt around her ankles.

Brianna can't believe what she's witnessing. Then a pair of red panties drop. Brianna thinks to herself, *'Oh my God, this bitch is getting undressed in my man's apartment!'* Then the woman climbs up onto the bed and lays there and starts to moan. Brianna realizes that the woman is masturbating on their new bed.

Brianna wants to climb out to confront the woman, but she is frozen by both fear and her own curiosity. She stays underneath the bed trying not to be heard. The fright of hiding under the bed knowing someone is only inches away masturbating, has a strange but erotically thrilling sensation about it. The longer Bri hides under the bed, her arousal intensifies, but she shakes it off by thinking about Bobby.

Suddenly, Bri's cell phone rings — she quickly grabs it and hits the answer button, but not before the woman hears it, jumps out of the bed, and drops to her knees to look underneath.

The woman yells, "YOU FREAK BITCH!! What the fuck are you doing under there?!" The woman reaches under the bed to pull Bri out by her arm as her phone drops to the floor.

Brianna stands up and looks the woman in the face for the first time. The woman is about ten years older than Bri and very attractive. She is taller than Brianna and about twenty-pounds thicker. The two of them start to scuffle with each other. Brianna pulls loose and steps back, "BOBBY IS MY MAN BITCH!!" right before lunging forward and punching the woman in her face, hard enough to knock her down to one knee.

"Now, get your shit and get out!"

The intruder staggers back to her feet then reaches for her skirt and panties. While frantically getting dressed the woman rushes to the front door repeating, "Okay, okay — I got you – okay bitch — I got you!" She grabs her shoes and a small black purse that she left sitting by the front door — then steps out into the breezeway.

Brianna yells, "AND DON'T EVER COME BACK HERE AGAIN!"

The stranger stands there for a brief moment with her back to the apartment door, then desperately reaches into her purse and pulls out a small handgun. From only five-feet away, she wildly turns and points the gun at Brianna's face and pulls the trigger twice — both times missing Bri's head by inches.

Instinctually Brianna grabs the sides of the door frame and thrusts forward, drop-kicking the woman in her chest. The woman stumbles backwards and falls down the flight of stairs. She lands unconscious on the concrete walkway below, dropping the gun on the way down. Scared of what to do next, Brianna runs back in the apartment, locks the door, and retrieves her phone. Bobby is still on the line, already in his car on his way to the apartment.

After hearing the loud echoes from the gun shots, multiple tenants in the building call the police. By the time Bobby pulls up, there are already seven police cars and an ambulance at the apartment complex.

The woman is on a stretcher at the bottom of the stairs. She has multiple broken bones from the fall. Bobby briefly glares at her as he runs up the stairs to his unit.

Two police officers are in the apartment living room talking to Brianna while another two are taking photos and digging the stray bullets out of the wall. When Bobby walks in, Brianna tells the police who he is. The police ask Bobby to wait in the hallway for a few more minutes. When the police finish talking with Brianna, they ask her to step outside so that they can talk to Bobby separately about his connection to the woman at the bottom of the stairs.

Bobby explains to the police that she is an ex-girlfriend that he has not seen in a long time. He also tells the officers that she called the other night while he and Bri were having dinner, but he never returned her call.

After thirty-minutes of private questioning, the police leave and tell Brianna she can go back into the apartment with Bobby.

Bobby has a stoic look on his face, "Get dressed, we're going to go get something to eat and then go up to the hospital!"

Brianna is upset that Bobby wants to go to the hospital. In her mind, *this is an evil woman that just tried to kill her — and now Bobby wants to visit her and see how she is doing?* But Brianna tries to stay open-minded, realizing that Bobby must have known her for many years.

They are both quiet in the car. They stop to get a bite to eat without talking much. After eating they drive around for a while longer to pass time. Bobby tells Bri they need to be at the hospital this evening at *8:30 pm sharp.*

***

Outside the hospital room, Officer Sanchez greets the couple as they come up the hallway, "Hello Mr. Robert King! *We've* been waiting for you — please go right in."

"Can my fiancé join me?" Bobby says.

"Yes — she certainty can!"

The couple step into the shadowy hospital room and stop just inside the door to look around. The darkness and faint beeps coming from the patient monitors are making Bri feel more uneasy than she already was. The only light in the room is from a dim fluorescent fixture mounted on the wall just above the hospital bed. A heavy gray curtain down the center of the room is blocking the view to any windows that might be on the other side.

The woman is asleep. Her neck is in a brace keeping her head from turning. One arm is in a full cast. She has a blood-stained gauze bandage wrapped around her forehead, partially covering one eye.

Bobby whispers very quietly to Brianna, *"Babe, go over there where she can't see you — I'll explain later."*

Reluctantly, Brianna steps out of sight and sits down in a chair located in the darkest corner of the room.

Bobby slowly steps closer to the bed, *"Trish, Trish — psst, wake up... It's Bobby!"*

She slowly opens her one uncovered eye and mumbles, "Bobby, is that you?"

"Yeah — it's me. How are you feeling?"

She grunts, "How in the fuck do you think I'm feeling?!" she takes a deep breath and continues, "your little nasty hood-rat bitch kicked me down the stairs!"

Brianna starts to get out of the chair, but Bobby turns and glares at her. He cuts his eyes as if to say, *'sit your ass back down!'*

Bobby quickly looks back at Trish, "Why did she kick you down the stairs?"

Trish mumbles, "Because I tried to kill the little bitch! She's lucky I missed! I tried to shoot the bitch in her ugly face!"

Bobby takes a deep breath, "Trisha — are you sure about what you are saying?"

"YES! And just wait till I heal — I'm coming to get that little bitch! Next time I won't miss!"

Brianna is shaking in her seat with anger.

Bobby looks down at Trish and takes her by the hand, "I don't understand how you got in my apartment. How did you get in?"

"Years ago, I made a copy of your spare key when I left to go pick up rental movies..." she pauses, "but what's with all the damn questions?"

Bobby turns and reaches out to Brianna. He gestures for her to come to his side. He looks back at Trish, "This is my everything! I can't let you hurt her — ever!" Without saying another word, he clenches Brianna's hand and turns to walk out the room.

"FUCK YOU BOBBY! — FUCK YOU and that little BITCH!"

Bobby and Brianna step out into the hallway. Just then all the lights in the hospital room come on and the gray curtain down the center quickly pulls back revealing a second officer holding a tape recorder and note pad.

Police Lieutenant Taun Nguyen approaches the bed side, "Ms. Trisha Franklin-Smith, based on your uncoerced confession — you are under arrest for unlawful entry, attempted murder, and continued death threats. At this time, you have the right to remain silent. Anything you say — can and will be used against you in a court of law. Do you understand your rights?"

Lieutenant Nguyen handcuffs one of Trisha's wrists to the arm rail as she screams as loud as she can, "GOD DAMMIT BOBBY!! YOU FUCKIN ASSHOLE! — I HOPE YOU FUCKING BURN IN HELL!!"

Just outside the hospital room, Officer Sanchez closes the door as soon as the couple step into the hallway. Then he reaches out to shake Bobby's hand, "Thank you for your help Mr. King. I know that wasn't easy."

Bobby pulls Brianna close, "I'll do anything for my woman. Nobody will ever try to hurt her and get away with it! – Nobody!"

Ch. 8 - Diamonds

Several weeks have passed — the shooting at the apartment is now just a bad memory. Now that the winter holidays are soon approaching, Bobby asks Brianna if she would like to stay in Seattle for Thanksgiving or go visit her friends and family in Los Angeles. Brianna tells Bobby that part of the reason she moved to Seattle was because she can only take small doses of her hood before she has to get away.

At Brianna's family gatherings, there is always alcohol, weed, loud music — and drama. It's common for gang members and street hustlers to show up. Whereas Bobby's family is far more conservative — no intoxicants of any kind, just folks talking, eating, and watching TV.

"Bobby, I want to meet your family."

"Okay babe, I'd like that!" he smiles.

Brianna has always been curious about Bobby's past, but never asked questions. When they pillow talk, Brianna is doing most of the sharing. But now that she is planning to spend the rest of her life with him, she would like to know more. Besides, she wants to know if there are any other women with guns that are going to try to kill her.

***

It's Thanksgiving morning. Brianna gets up early to make a meatless spinach lasagna to take to Bobby's family gathering. She is excited and nervous at the same time. After putting the food in the oven, she steps into the bathroom to start getting ready. Bobby cleans up the kitchen and loads the dishwasher. He makes sure not to start the wash cycle yet so that Bri has plenty of hot water for her shower. He sits on the couch flipping through college football games on TV until Brianna comes out.

She steps out of the bedroom in a pink, tight-fitting tee, designer jeans, and carrying a pair of low-cut black dress boots. She's accessorized her outfit with five-inch hoop earrings, a black velvet choker and silver ringlets at the ends of her two braids. She sets down her boots by the front door and walks into the kitchen, "Babe, what do you think — is this okay to wear?"

Bobby's eyes light up, "Daaamn babe — you are tooo hot!!"

She blushes, "Whatever — not as hot as you Mr. Handsome!"

"You look perfect!"

"Thank you babe."

With a mischievous grin Bobby adds, "...and I like that *choker* — very sexy!" then growls under his breath.

Bri laughs, "It was either this choker, or makeup to cover my tat — and since I don't have any makeup this had to do."

"You know you don't need to cover your tattoo — right?"

"Yeah I guess so — but I want to. And one day I'm going to get it removed."

Bobby smiles — then turns to open the oven.

"So, how's the food look Bobby?"

"Perfect timing, it's 10:30 and the lasagna just got done — so we can head out now."

They grab everything and head out the door like a well-organized team. Bobby carries the hot dish down to the car as Brianna opens the back passenger-side door and lays out a large towel across the back seat. Then Bobby reaches in and places the pan, making sure it won't slide around during the drive.

After securing the food, Bobby opens Brianna's door for her. She gets in and stretches over to unlock the driver's side door — revealing her lower back and the top of her black lace panties. He stays put for a moment, taking advantage of the view before walking around and getting in.

On the drive to his parents' house, the couple has an intimate talk as always.

"Bobby, I'm so happy to be able to spend our first holiday together. I hope I don't say anything wrong in front of your family."

"Just be yourself — my family will love you the way you are. We are going to have a great time."

Right after Bobby graduated from high school his mom and dad moved out of the low-income housing projects that Bobby was raised in — to a house in the suburbs. They now live in the small town of Kenmore, about a thirty-mile drive north of Seattle.

As they get closer to their destination Bobby says, "We are almost there — I'm starving!"

"Me too! We should've put the lasagna in the trunk, the smell is torturing me."

They both laugh.

Then Brianna stops suddenly and turns to Bobby, "Oh my goodness babe, I don't know your parents' names — what should I call them when we get there?"

Bobby grins, "Brenda and Floyd."

"I love that, *Brenda and Floyd,* it has a nice ring to it."

"Yep, that's my parents, they're quite a team," he chuckles. "Well we're here!"

They turn off the street, and down a long private driveway that leads to an older country-style house, surrounded by tall, evergreen trees. There are more than a dozen cars parked out front and a few in the grass.

They park and grab the food out of the back seat.

"I love your parents' house. It's so secluded."

Bobby smiles, "Yeah, Pops calls it his little country castle in the forest!"

They both laugh and walk up to the porch.

When they step through the doorway, they are greeted with lots of smiles and waves. It's an open space house with very few interior walls. From the entry way they can see folks mingling in the large living room, the kitchen, and the dining room. There must be close to thirty or more people in all. Brianna notices that it's an older crowd and everyone is dressed more conservatively than she is — one of the gentlemen is even wearing a suit and tie.

Both Bobby's mom and dad immediately stop what they're doing and rush to the front door. His mom is a tall, elegant woman with dark chocolate skin and silver hair. She is wearing a long black evening gown and covered in huge diamonds. Bobby's dad is a short, caramel complexion man with a thick mustache and mini-afro. He's wearing a black retro Adidas sweatsuit with white stripes.

The two of them look good together. Brianna can sense their young spirits.

Bobby's mom pulls him in tight and kisses him, then reaches out to Brianna and draws her in for a hug as well, placing a warm kiss on her cheek.

Bobby's dad gives his son a hug, then embraces Brianna the same way and smiles, "Ms. Brianna, make yourself at home. If you need anything just go find it — *mi casa es su casa*." Then he turns and skirmishes back into the living room to watch football with a few of the others.

Brianna almost tears up from the affectionate greeting she just received. She recalls that her family is not as nice to strangers.

Bobby's mom reaches out, "Baby girl, let me take your coat and hang it up."

Feeling awkward and under dressed, Brianna hesitantly gives up her coat, revealing her cute figure, tight jeans — and no bra. Several heads turn, with lots of smiles from the guys, and a couple of smirks and eye rolls from the women.

Bobby's mother senses Brianna is a bit uncomfortable and lets her know her outfit is perfectly fine, "Gurrrl, if I had a body like that, I would show it off too!"

Brianna blushes, grabs Bobby's hand tight for comfort and whispers in his ear, *"I love your mom."*

Bobby takes Brianna and walks her around the house introducing her to everyone. Lots of hugs are exchanged.

As time passes, Brianna relaxes. She even breaks away from Bobby a few times to talk to different relatives one-on-one. She is eager to get to know Bobby's family — all of them.

Bobby's older brother Mark is standing in the kitchen having a beer while people watching. Mark is a carpenter — he's 6'-5" and was once the star linebacker on his high school football team. Brianna approaches him and starts a conversation.

While Brianna is standing in the kitchen next to Mark, the conversation turns to how the new couple met. Brianna briefly tells the story of the airport meeting without going into details.

In a husky voice Mark says, "You're way different from all of the women my brother has dated in the past. He mostly dates those stuffy — professional type females with lots of money."

Brianna gives Mark an awkward stare, then looks down.

Mark realizes his words may not have come out right, "Sis, don't take that the wrong way. I hate those kinds of fake-ass broads. I just met you, and I already like you much better than *any* of his other girlfriends!"

Brianna gives Mark a bashful smile.

Then Mark asks, "So, what type of men have you typically dated in the past?"

Without much thought, Brianna quickly answers, "Bobby is my first!"

Mark blurts out, "Are you a lesbian or something?" then starts laughing.

Heads turn in the room as folks overhear Mark's question. Now there are multiple people waiting for Bri's next response.

Brianna stays true to herself and says with confidence, "As a matter fact — I *was* gay until I met Bobby."

There's another awkward pause. Brianna looks around the room full of stares in her direction. She makes direct eye contact with Jill, Bobby's older sister. Jill is sitting in a nearby recliner with her mother's white cat sitting in her lap. Jill is a younger carbon copy of her mom, minus the silver hair.

While slowly petting the cat, she proudly lifts her chin, "I know that's right girlfriend — my little brother is a one-of-a-kind man, he could make *any* woman fall in love with him!"

Brianna smiles and nods in agreement and turns back to Bobby's brother.

Mark grins, "Yep, that's my little bro — he's one lovable motherfucker!"

At that moment Brianna starts to laugh with happiness. She feels like she's with people she can trust. People she can be herself with. She feels like she's with her new family.

Bobby walks up and says, "Y'all are having a lot of fun — what are we talking about?"

Brianna giggles, "Oh nothing, I'll tell you later babe."

"Okay — well I'm about to run to the 24-hour mini-mart and pick up some more beverages, we're running low. Why don't you stay here with my family — I'll be right back."

Brianna agrees. Bobby walks towards the door, but before opening it, he turns back around and blows Brianna a kiss. She's silently mouths back, *'I love you babe!'*

After Bobby walks out the door, Mark gives Brianna a warm smile and asks, "So, are you enjoying yourself?"

She responds, "Very much! Everybody is so nice, and your mother is so beautiful. She looks like a movie star with all those *diamonds*!"

Mark laughs and blurts out, "She got all those diamonds because my dad used to fuck up a lot!"

Brianna looks confused, "What do you mean by — *your dad used to fuck up a lot??*"

"All those diamonds she wears — well every time my dad would fuck up he would buy my mom *diamonds*." Mark laughs again and continues, "See, we grew up poor in Seattle, we lived in government housing and my dad used to run the streets. Because we stayed in such a tight-knit neighborhood, nothing stayed a secret for long. So, when my dad picked up a little *side-piece* here and there, the word would eventually get back to my mom. She would take all of his shit and throw it outside in the front yard for the whole neighborhood to see. She used to stand in the doorway with a butcher knife and dare him to try to get back in the house. My dad would pick up his shit from the ground and find somewhere else to go for a few days — or at least until my mom cooled off a little. Well, one day after fucking up, pops came home with a diamond bracelet and got down on his knees in the front yard and begged for forgiveness. My mom stood on the porch staring at him like he had lost his mind. She stepped down from the porch and held the tip of her knife to my dad's throat while she snatched the bracelet. Then my mom looked around to see who was watching and told him to pick up his shit and get in the house."

Brianna's eyes are wide open as she listens to Mark continue with his story. In the back of her mind she's hoping that Bobby hasn't taken on any of his dad's traits.

Mark continues with his story, "Yep, it was those diamonds that got that dude back in the house, so he continued to use *diamonds* as get-out-of-jail-free cards — and he continued to fuck up. But each time he did, he stayed true to his pattern to bring home more diamonds. After a while it became the family inside-joke. Anytime my mom would show up at a holiday party with new diamonds, the family knew pops had been fucking up again!"

With deep concern Brianna asks, "Does your dad still run the streets like he did back in the day?"

"Oh, hell naw! That shit ended a long time ago! One day pops came home from one of his many *Sexcapades* with a big grin on his face and holding a jewelry box. My mom damn near ripped the front door off its hinges as she yanked it open and ran out on to the porch. With red eyes and tears streaming down her cheeks, she shouted at the top of her lungs, *'I have all the jewelry a bitch could ever wear!! What I need now is a faithful husband — or I will settle for a dead one!!'* Then my mom pulled out a nickel plated *.357* revolver and pointed it at my father's forehead. She cried, *'If you ever cheat on me again don't come home. If you do, I will kill you right here in this front yard for the* *world to see!'* — Everything changed that very moment. Pops was a new man from that day forward and he stopped running the streets. Now all he does is go to work and come straight home to mama!" Mark laughs and continues, "The family joke is — he saw his life flash in front of his face, literally. So, my mom still sports those diamonds with pride every chance she gets. She tells people that she went through a lot of pain and suffering for those diamonds, and she ain't giving them up for nothing!"

Brianna stares at Mark and asks, "Do you think she would have really shot your dad?"

"Oh, hell yeah! — I was just a kid at the time, but I will *never* forget that look in my mom's eyes."

Brianna thinks to herself; she has just been initiated into the family after hearing that very personal and dramatic story. She empathizes with Bobby's mother's past pain through Mark's words.

***

It's pitch-dark outside and raining hard. There's no traffic on the neighborhood side roads because of the holiday. About a half-mile before Bobby reaches the convenience store, a husky woman with long dirty blonde hair and rain-soaked clothing suddenly appears in his headlights. She's walking slowly along the sidewalk on the right, in the same direction that he's driving. She has no coat on and is dangling a pair of high heal shoes in one hand. Just as Bobby is about to drive past her, she loses her footing and stumbles into the street — right in front of his car.

He SLAMS on his brakes!!

She regains her footing, steps back onto the sidewalk, and continues strolling. Under the glow of the streetlamp above Bobby can see she's intoxicated. Out of natural concern, he pulls forward slowly, rolls down his passenger side window and asks, "Lady, are you okay?"

She stumbles over to the car, leans in the window and slurs, "My feet hurt. Can you give me a ride — just up the street?"

Bobby's protective nature surfaces. He thinks to himself, *'It's the holiday, it's dark, it's raining and she's a woman. I can't just drive past not knowing if she makes it to her destination safe or not.'*

He decides to give the woman a ride, "Okay, get in!"

She quickly grabs for the handle before he can change his mind. She flops into the passenger seat and slams the door behind her. Immediately Bobby notices the odor of alcohol, urine, and cigarettes — along with the stench of her dirty rain-soaked hair. She smells like she hasn't bathed in days. Bobby cracks his window to get a breeze of fresh air, and immediately regrets offering her a ride.

Placing one hand over his mouth and nose he asks, "Okay — where are you going?"

She slurs, "Just up the street," and slaps the palm of her large hand on the dashboard.

Bobby starts driving for a few blocks and looks over at her again, "HEY! Wake-up! — Where do you want me to let you off?"

Slumped back in the seat as if she's about to snooze off, she screams like a demon, "SHUT UP NIGGER! — Just keep driving till I tell you to stop!"

"Oh, hell NO! You're getting out NOW!"

"STOP talking to me you black fucker! — You're making my fucking head hurt!"

An anger builds inside of Bobby like he's never felt before — he regrets trying to be helpful. He looks around to see where he can pull over to let her out. He sees a small white church up ahead with curbside parking and a few streetlamps lighting up the sidewalk.

He pulls over to the curb and puts the car in park, "Get out — NOW!"

With drooped eyelids she slurs, "FUCK YOU! — I'm ain't going anywhere!"

Feeling an anxiety to get back to Brianna, he doesn't think things through. He lets his anger override his logic. He doesn't want to have to explain to Brianna why he was picking up a strange woman walking down the street at night. Instead of stepping out of his car and calling the police, he decides to take things into his own hands.

Bobby opens his car door and steps out into the rain. While rushing around to the passenger side he glances through the rain-soaked windshield and sees the distorted image of the woman staring back at him. Before he makes it to the other side, she locks the doors. Bobby leans over and looks in. Panic surfaces as he realizes he's left the keys in the ignition and his phone in the cup holder. Standing in the rain he pounds on the glass with the side of his fist, "OPEN THE DOOR!! GET OUT!!!"

The two of them exchange glares as Bobby's mind races to find his next move.

Without warning, there's a bright burst of light followed by two short siren blasts. From a loudspeaker a man yells, "PUT YOUR HANDS UP WHERE I CAN SEE THEM!"

Bobby didn't notice the police car when it pulled up. Squinting into the bright light Bobby raises his hands and yells back to the cop, "This crazy woman won't get out my car!"

"KEEP YOUR HANDS UP AND SLOWLY GET ON YOUR KNEES!" the officer commands.

"I didn't do anything wrong!" Bobby pleads as he kneels to the ground.

"SIR — DO NOT — MAKE ANY SUDDEN MOVES!!" the officer yells.

Bobby does as he's instructed. He gets down on his knees in the rain next to the car, being careful not to move too quickly.

With the spotlight blinding Bobby's sight, he can barely make out a silhouette of a police officer stepping out of his squad car with a gun raised. The officer slowly walks towards Bobby then quickly pulls Bobby's wrists behind his head and cuffs him tightly, "Now stay there! DON'T MOVE!"

Then the cop yells for the woman to roll down the window and stay in the car. Although she's intoxicated, she's able to fully comply. Then he tells her to turn off the car, take the keys out the ignition and drop them out the window onto the ground. The officer kicks the keys to the side, then asks Bobby where his driver's license is. Bobby tells the officer his wallet is inside his inner jacket pocket — on the left side. The police bends and reaches into Bobby's coat while holding the gun to his back. The officer asks the woman for her identification. She says she doesn't have any.

Bobby tries to explain to the police that he just met the woman and was only trying to help her get out of the rain, and off the street safely. The officer instructs the woman to stay in the car and not move. The cop pulls Bobby to his feet then escorts him back to the squad car and shoves him into the back seat.

***

It's been thirty-minutes since Bobby left his parents' house. Brianna is getting worried. She calls his phone, but it just rings until the voicemail greeting comes on. Brianna knows something's wrong. Bobby always picks up her calls — even when he's at work.

Brianna finds Mark and asks him to drive her to go look for Bobby. At first, Mark shrugs it off and jokingly says, "He's probably taking the scenic route."

When Mark sees the seriousness on Brianna's face, he grabs his hat and coat and says, "Come on let's go! I know my brother — I know the route he takes to the store!"

As the two hurry toward the front door Bobby's mom says, "Drive safe — call me if you need to!"

"We will Momma!" Mark stops and kisses his mom on the cheek before darting down the driveway to meet Brianna already standing at his orange pickup truck.

During the drive Mark does his best to calm Brianna down, "I know my bro — if anything was wrong, he would have called right away."

With panic in her voice she says, "What if he's hurt and can't call?"

Mark looks straight ahead with a blank face and keeps driving. The windshield wipers toss sheets of rain from side-to-side as they drive down the dark, empty streets.

"THERE!!" Brianna screams, "Up ahead!!"

The police car spotlight is still shining through Bobby's back window. At first, they don't see Bobby, only the back of the woman's head still sitting in Bobby's car. Brianna thinks to herself, *'What the fuck is going on here?'*

Mark slowly pulls up behind the police car, making sure not to startle anyone. He turns off his headlights, leaving only the amber parking lights on, then rolls down his window and yells, "That's my little brother's car! We are worried — can I please step out of my truck officer?"

The police officer yells back, "Both of you — put your hands where I can see them and walk around to the front of your truck — slowly!"

As Mark and Brianna get out, they hear a female dispatcher's voice announce over the officer's walkie-talkie, *"Male suspect is all clear — no priors — over-and-out."*

Brianna stops at the police car and stares into Bobby's blank face through the window.

"Ma'am step away from the squad car!" the officer instructs.

Brianna quickly turns away, and catches up to Mark as he introduces himself to the officer while showing his driver's license and veteran military ID.

After a few minutes, the officer pulls Bobby from the back seat and removes the handcuffs from his wrists. He gives Bobby his wallet and keys back. The cop tells the three of them to get in Mark's truck and drive off.

The officer says, "You can come back and get the car in twenty-minutes, after backup arrives and we take this woman away. She is a notorious prostitute in the area, known for robbing unsuspecting men who pick her up." The officer concludes with, "If Bobby had only good intentions — he's lucky I showed up when I did. She's also known to carry a concealed knife."

Brianna hears all of this and starts shaking. The three of them climb into Mark's truck, Brianna in the middle. They drive to a nearby bank parking lot to wait out the time until the police are done.

With red eyes, Brianna blurts out, "So, what the FUCK happened?"

Mark says, "I'll step out of the truck so you two can talk in private."

"No — stay here bro!"

Bobby tells the entire story from the beginning — until the point when Mark and Bri pull up behind the police car. When Bobby is done telling what happened Brianna leans back and punches him in his shoulder as hard as she can, "Don't you ever pick up any strange bitches EVER again! YOU HERE ME!!!"

Bobby's face drops, "I won't babe — I promise!"

The three of them sit in silence for a few more minutes before going back to get Bobby's car.

***

Back at the spot where he was pulled over, Bobby's car is sitting with the passenger window still down. The leather seat is wet from the rain. Bobby opens his trunk and pulls out a large towel and some spray cleaner. He tells Mark to go ahead back home and let everyone know things are okay — and to let his mom know that they will be there soon. Mark drives off.

"Bri, I have to scrub down the seat before I can allow you to get in the car — that tramp smelled like a wet dog."

They both start to laugh as Brianna jumps in the driver's seat to get out of the rain, "Give me the keys so I can roll up the window and get the heat going."

After scrubbing deep into the seams, Bobby feels it's clean enough. He tosses the towel into the trunk then walks over to the driver's door and opens it, "Okay baby, it's ready for you. The seat is clean as new."

Bri grins, "Nope I'm not sitting over there, get your ass in the passenger seat — I'm driving!"

Bobby laughs and does what he's told. He buckles up for the ride.

***

Back at his parents' house they have a wonderful time the rest of the evening. It was the most exciting Thanksgiving Brianna or Bobby have ever had. At one-point during the party Brianna steps away to visit the restroom. When she returns she whispers in Bobby's ear, *"Wait till we get home, I'm going to fuck you good tonight!"* then takes Bobby's hand and places her panties in his palm. His eyes open wide as she bashfully looks around to see if anyone saw the exchange.

***

On the ride back to the apartment, Brianna can't keep her hands off of Bobby as he drives. As soon as he parks the car, she jumps out and runs up the stairs. She pushes open the front door, kicks off her shoes and strips on the way to the bedroom. Completely undressed, she dives up on the bed and bounces, "Get your ass in here babe! I'm going to give you something special!"

Bobby walks in the room with a huge grin on his face and slowly removes his clothes while adoring Brianna's alluring friskiness.

She giggles and tugs at Bobby to get up on the bed. Without wasting any time, she pushes him down on his back while putting his shaft in her warm mouth. Her plan is to take Bobby to ecstasy — but he has something else in mind.

Bobby places his hand on her hip to rotate her around in the *69* position — so that she is straddling his face. He lets out moans of enjoyment as he kisses and licks every spot he can reach. He makes her feel so good she can barely concentrate on what she's doing. Eventually she stops pleasuring him and lays her head on his thigh while clenching the sheets in her fists.

She can feel her orgasm building to the point of eruption. She digs her nails into the bed as she tries to pull up from his hot mouth, but his hold is too strong. Bobby concentrates on a spot that he hopes will send her over the edge. He lightly wiggles the tip of his tongue until she cannot hold back any longer. She explodes on his face. She can hear him lapping up her juices like a thirsty beast.

Panting and almost breathless, Brianna pushes out, "Oh my god babe — how did you get so fuckin' good at that?"

From between her legs — he whispers, *"I listen to you and pay close attention to what makes you feel good..."*

Ch. 9 - New Neighbor

It's a blue-sky Saturday morning in early December — five-months since the couple first met.

Over breakfast Bobby asks, "Have you ever thought about *us* getting married?"

Brianna's eyes open wide, "Don't tease me like that!"

"Babe, I'm not teasing with you! So, tell me, do you ever think about it?"

Her eyes start to water, "Uh yeah — all day, every day!"

"Are you serious?"

"Yes, I'm totally serious! I want you and only you — I will do anything for you!"

Bobby smiles, "I feel the same way!"

They talk it through and agree not to rush things, but marriage is now their ultimate goal.

After eating and getting dressed, they decide to go for a stroll at a nearby beach before running a few weekend errands. They plan on stopping for groceries on the way back home.

As they head out for the day, they pause just outside their front door before going down the stairs to the parking lot. There is a new female tenant coming up carrying a box. She's tall, in her thirties and has a smooth dark chocolate complexion. She is wearing sweats and a baseball cap.

Bobby speaks first, "Hi, welcome to the building."

The woman barely glances at him from under her visor but lifts her chin and stares straight into Brianna's eyes — then slips in a wink, and whispers, *"Hi!"* as she enters the unit directly across the hall from them.

The couple continue down the stairs and walk to the car.

Bobby opens Bri's door. As she's getting in, she turns back and says, "I don't like the way that bitch looked at me!"

"You noticed that too?" Bobby replies and walks over to the driver's side and gets in.

"Yes, so disrespectful! She saw I was with you. I can tell I'm going to have words with that trifling bitch at some point. I've run into her type before."

"Don't even sweat it babe — she's just a squirrel tryin' to get a nut!"

They both laugh and go on about their Saturday without bringing up the new neighbor again.

***

When they return to the apartment late that afternoon, the new neighbor has her front door wide open while unpacking. She has changed into booty shorts and a white tank top. Both Bobby and Brianna can't help but notice the new neighbor's nice body as they carry groceries into the apartment.

As they begin to put the groceries away, Brianna says, "I'm about to go tell that bitch to close her fuckin' door!"

"Babe, let it go — we have bigger things to think about — besides, she ain't shit anyway!"

"You're right Bobby, I'll try to ignore her."

"Besides Bri, I've been waiting for the perfect opportunity to buy a house and get away from this ghetto ass apartment complex. This is a sign that it's time to make it happen. I have a real estate agent that has been occasionally sending me house listings — but now I'm ready to take it more seriously. I want you to be a part of the final decision making."

Brianna can't believe what she's hearing. She thinks to herself, *whenever something bad happens, Bobby always comes to the rescue and surprises her with something good.*

***

The following week the couple drive around after work looking at houses from the agent's listing. After driving past fifteen houses that night, they pull up to a small, sky-blue rambler with white trim. Although it's dark outside, the second Brianna sees it, she knows it's the one.

Bobby glances at the detail sheet he printed at work, "This house is very affordable — it's priced for a quick sale. I'll schedule an appointment with the agent first thing in the morning so we can see the inside of it."

The next day, they meet up with the real estate agent and drive out to look at the house again. As they open the door and walked in, both of them envision themselves living there. The house is an older one with hardwood oak floors and a brick fireplace. It appears to be in excellent condition, having both the kitchen and single bathroom being recently updated. It has a small front yard, but the huge, fenced in backyard makes up for what's lacking out front. It's located in a quiet neighborhood where all the other yards are well-kept.

Bobby pulls Brianna to the side and whispers, *"Babe, if you like this one, I'll have the agent make an offer."*

Brianna tiptoes and kisses Bobby on the cheek, "This house is perfect!"

***

For the next two-weeks the agent diligently works on the house deal. The couple's offer is accepted, and they move forward with the closing process. Bobby's finances are in good order, so the deal goes through quickly, and without a hitch.

Bobby arranges to take the last week of December and the first week of January off work so they can settle into the new house. Bri's job also let her take a few days off for the move.

It's just four days before Christmas. There is a lot to get done in the next few days. The two of them work as a team to get ready for the move. Brianna does all the packing and finds a reputable moving company, while Bobby concentrates on communicating with the real estate agent and making sure his bank has everything they need in a timely manner. He also works on things like, change of addresses, and turning on utilities at the new house. Together, they go shopping for Persian rugs for the hardwood floors and schedule them to be delivered the day of the move.

The house sale closes on the afternoon of December 22, and they pick up the keys to be ready for the big move the next morning.

At 8:00 am December 23, Bobby supervises the moving crew back at the apartment while

Brianna is already over at the new house cleaning it from top to bottom. She wipes down all the cabinets, and dust-mops the oak floors before the new rugs arrive.

After the movers have fully loaded the truck back at the apartment, Bobby and the crew set off for the new house to meet Brianna. Just before noon Bobby drives up with the moving truck right behind him. Brianna runs out and greets him with a big kiss before showing the movers where things should go. She doesn't want the movers to step on the new rugs other than to set the large furniture in its designated places. She instructs the movers to stack all of the boxes in the small dining room against the walls. The couple will take things into the appropriate rooms themselves.

The couple work continuously throughout the day and late into the night, unpacking and arranging as they go — barely stopping for breaks. Bobby passes out on the couch by midnight, but Brianna is so ecstatic that she'll never have to look at the old apartment again, sleep is the last thing on her mind. She continues working by herself until the very last thing is unpacked, each electronic is connected, and everything has a new place. She finishes by 1:00 am and steps in to their new bathroom to take the best shower of her life, while making sure to leave enough hot water for Bobby if he wants to wash up before bed. After her shower she sets out a towel on the vanity for Bobby and walks into the living room to wake him up. After his shower they both pass out like bears in hibernation as soon as the hit the bed.

Sleeping in late the next morning, Brianna is the first to wake. She looks around the room. She just lays there taking it all in. It's a wonderful feeling knowing that they are completely settled in their new home — and it's Christmas Eve.

Brianna nudges Bobby to wake him, "Babe — baby, can we get a Christmas tree? Pretty please?"

"Okay babe — I saw a place selling Christmas trees just about five miles from here. Let's get up and go before they close."

After getting dressed, the couple jump in the car and go out to find a tree. They pull up to Carpinito Brothers produce stand, converted to a Christmas tree outlet for the season. There aren't many cars parked in the lot, and only a few customers browsing the last remains of the seasonal inventory.

"Bobby, what do you think of the flocked trees that look like they're covered in snow?"

"I love 'em — my mom always liked flocked trees!"

Brianna smiles, "I really like your mom, she has great taste!"

The couple exchange thoughts on what makes a good tree, and together decide on the perfect one. Now to get it tied to the top of Bobby's car for the drive home.

One of the Carpinito brothers comes over and helps by providing a thick, clear-plastic sheet to lay over the top of the car. He spreads out the plastic to make sure the tree does not scratch the paint while doing a careful job securing it to the roof.

As Bobby is working with the attendant to load the tree, Brianna grabs a tree stand, a few sets of lights and some ornaments to take to the cashier near the exit of the yard.

The yard also sells firewood logs, so Bobby asks the man to toss in a few bundles. The gentleman lays down plastic in Bobby's trunk, loads the wood and writes down the total on a yellow sticky note to take to the cashier. Bobby smiles, hands the man a $40 tip and says, "Merry Christmas!"

"Thank You! — and Merry Christmas to you and your wife!"

Bobby walks over to the cashier where Brianna is standing, "Bri, the man told me to tell my wife Merry Christmas — So Merry Christmas babe!"

Bri giggles, "So — I'm your wife now? — just like that? Well I'm going to have to thank that man on the way out."

As the couple walk back to the car, Brianna detours over to the man that loaded the tree and says, "Merry Christmas to you, and your family sir! — and thank you for your help!"

***

That evening back at the new house Bobby puts a few logs on the fire to set the mood while Brianna makes spiced hot chocolate. Once the fire is roaring Bobby relaxes on the couch enjoying his holiday drink and adoring Brianna as she decorates the tree. She takes her time arranging ornaments and lights so that the tree has good balance.

It's a romantic evening. The fireplace is burning, and the TV is playing Christmas movies in the background. During a commercial break, the local news mentions it will snow throughout the night. The couple sleep with the bedroom blinds wide open to watch the snow fall against the moonlit sky.

***

The next morning is the couple's first Christmas together — they get out of bed before the sun rises and bundle up for an early morning walk. They step out on the front porch to find 4-inches of snow covering everything in sight. Still dark outside, the light from the streetlamps cast white circles on the sidewalks as they explore the neighborhood — they are the first to leave their footprints in the freshly fallen snow.

"Bri, let's stroll down this hill and see where it leads."

Full of holiday spirit Brianna giggles, "Okay babe, just as long as we *find our way back home*."

At the bottom of the hill they discover a small neighborhood park surrounded by snow frosted evergreen trees. The couple hold hands as they follow a pathway that twists its way to a clearing in the center of the park. In the middle they find a small duck pond that is covered with a thin sheet of ice. There isn't anyone around, it's totally silent and everything is white. The romantic landscape looks like something you would see in an oil painting.

They stand there for a few minutes taking in nature's beauty and the early morning silence. Then Bobby turns to Brianna and takes her hands. He looks into her eyes as he slowly goes down on one knee. He reaches into his pocket.

Bobby pulls out a huge diamond ring and kisses the back of her hand, "Brianna, will you please marry me?"

Shocked by the unexpected gesture, her voice cracks, "Oh my god Bobby! — this is too much — I don't deserve all this — you are too good to me!" Tears start to run down her cheeks as she lowers herself and embraces him with a tight hug and deep kiss, "Yes — yes — yes!! — of course I will marry you!! Yes!!"

They both stay on their knees holding each other for a few minutes. Then Bobby pulls back and slides the warm ring that he has been clenching in his palm onto her cold finger. She glances at the ring and says, "It's perfect babe — just like us!"

Brianna pulls Bobby to the ground. The two of them roll in the snow kissing and laughing.

Ch. 10 - Spaghetti Dinner

A month after the couple move into the new house and get engaged — life for them both is going great. During dinner, the subject of wedding plans comes up. Without any disagreement, they both decide they will get married in July — one year after they first met.

Brianna asks, "Babe, can we have a housewarming party soon? We can also announce our engagement to the family."

"That's a great idea Bri!"

"Bobby, I have been thinking — I also want to go to school. Since we are getting married, I would like to be able to bring more to the table."

"Okay babe, but you are going to need your own car if you are going to be working and going to school. Let's go car shopping next weekend."

***

They get up early the next Saturday morning and drive to the same Lexus dealer Bobby got his car from. Bobby knows one of the salesmen, and since he already bought one car from him, Bobby will leverage that to try to get a good deal on a second one.

Brianna suggests, "Bobby, maybe our second vehicle should be bigger so that we have something to pick up household supplies and anything else that would be too big for your trunk?"

"That's a great idea babe! — I totally agree."

They find a white two-year-old Lexus sport utility vehicle with low miles on it. Bri takes it for a test drive and loves it.

Bobby's credit score jumped up after purchasing the house so the car buying process goes quickly. On the drive home, Bobby lets Brianna lead the way in her new car while he follows. Along the way he takes a few photos of her driving with his cell phone.

They both pull into the driveway side by side. Bobby gets out of his car and rushes over to open Brianna's door for her. When he puts his hand on the handle, he sees her in the car with her hands over her face crying.

He opens the door, "baby, what's wrong?"

She lifts her head, "Babe, I know you're getting tired of me saying this, but this is all too good to be true sometimes," she sniffles and continues, "before I met you, my life didn't have any direction. I was just going day by day not knowing what was coming next. Now my life has purpose. There's a plan for my life. I owe that all to you."

He leans into the car and kisses her on the forehead, "Are you hungry? Let's go grab something to eat and talk." He walks around and gets in the passenger side.

As Brianna drives Bobby navigates her to a quiet, Italian restaurant a few miles away. As soon as they arrive, the host seats them in the back of the restaurant — in the booth they sit side by side. After ordering the food Bobby chooses to take advantage of this private moment to really express how much Bri means to him.

"Brianna baby, you say you now have a plan for your life, and you owe it to me? I feel the same way. I now have a plan for my life, and I owe that all to you!" Bobby slides closer to Brianna in the booth and continues, "Before I met you, I only dreamt about being in love. You made my dreams come true. Now I have something to truly live for. In the past, everything in the back of my mind was to prepare for the day I would meet you — the way I managed my finances, my health, and my love life. I purposely stayed single so that I would be ready for the woman of my dreams when she came into my life. On that first flight we shared down to LA, I fell in love with you. And although I doubted us many times in the very beginning, I caught myself, and pushed away any negative thoughts so that we could have the healthiest relationship possible."

Brianna gazes into Bobby's eyes as he continues to talk and express how deeply he is in love with her. She realizes at that moment — that no one has ever loved her before. What she thought was love, in the past, was actually obsession, or lust. But whatever it was, it certainly wasn't love. What she feels for Bobby, and what he feels for her is completely different.

She sniffles, "Babe, I love you so much!"

The waitress arrives with a single large plate of spaghetti and meatballs for the couple to share.

To prevent the waitress from thinking there is a problem, Brianna blurts out, "My man just bought me a car today — my tears are tears of joy!"

The waitress responds, "Sweetheart, you got a good man — don't ever let him go!"

Ch. 11 - Study Partner

Four more months have passed. Brianna has enrolled in a small local college for the Spring quarter. She is having a lot of fun on campus and is making a few new friends. In her business management class, the professor assigns a large project and announces that students will need to find a study partner to work with. Brianna glances around the classroom to see if there is any one that could make a good study companion.

On the far side of the classroom is a Latina named Lola. She has a nice smile and looks friendly. The two make eye contact and give each other a nod to confirm their study partnership.

After class, the two chat in the hallway and exchange numbers. Lola is short with a bubbly personality and plans to major in accounting.

Brianna and Lola start spending lots of time together studying. They both want to get a 'A' in this class. They text each other from time to time. Things are going good as a friendship. They even start to do things outside of school.

One Sunday evening before a big test, Brianna invites Lola over to the house to study together. Lola meets Bobby and they hit it off well. Bobby orders food for the ladies while they study in the dining room. He goes in the bedroom and closes the door to read. After studying for a few hours, Lola says that she needs to take a break. Brianna agrees and suggest they go sit on the couch and watch TV for a while.

While sitting on the couch Lola moves closer to Brianna and leans in for a kiss.

Bri jumps up and yells, "What the fuck are you doing BITCH?"

"I'm so sorry Breezy, I guess I read things wrong between us."

"You sure the fuck did! – It's time for you to GO!"

I'm sorry Breezy, it will never happen again."

"You're damn right it will never happen again! – and don't EVER call me Breezy again or I will punch your fucken lights out!"

Bobby hears the commotion and steps out of the bedroom just in time to see Lola leaving and Brianna slamming the door behind her.

"What happened babe?"

"That little bitch tried to kiss me!"

Bobby starts to laugh, "Oh that's all?"

Brianna looks at Bobby with an unamused expression, "I'm glad you think that shit's funny! She's lucky I didn't grab a knife out the kitchen and cut her ass!"

"Bri — I'm sure it's not the first time a girl made a pass at you, and I'm sure it won't be the last."

Brianna snarls, "Bobby — I'm really pissed right now — you better get on my side real soon and see it from my perspective!"

"I'm sorry babe, you're completely right, I would be pissed if I were in your shoes. Do you want to talk about it?"

"No — I just want to get some sleep so I am on point and get an 'A' on my test tomorrow. Then I won't have to interact with that flaky bitch ever again!"

Ch. 12 - The Bachelor Party

It's early July and a year since they met — the couples wedding is one week away. Brianna just got out of school last month for the start of summer break. She will return in September to continue her classes.

The couple agreed to have a private wedding with just immediate family and close friends. The ceremony is being held at Bobby's parents' house. The back yard is large enough to accommodate everyone and more. Currently there are seventy-five people on the invite list, but some are not expected to make it. Brianna has invited her mom, her younger brother Jimmy, and a few other close friends from California. So far none of Brianna's invites have confirmed their attendance other than Jimmy. He informs Bri that he'll try to fly up or take a train.

Ten of Bobby's closest friends decide to throw him a bachelor party on the Friday night before the wedding. The fellas are all hard working, 9 to 5 type guys. One is a city worker, another a bus driver and a few of them work for local tech companies.

They agree to have the party at Anthony's house. Anthony is one of the single guys of the group. It's a large two-story condo, not far from Bobby's old apartment. The gang starts showing up about 7:30 pm. There's plenty of beer, liquor, food, and music. The guys all pitch in and hire strippers from a local escort company.

As the fellas stand around laughing and talking about cars, sports, and women, the doorbell rings. One of the guys rushes to open it. Standing on the porch are two beautiful ladies in their twenties. One is tall, with coco-brown skin and wearing her hair in two afro-puffs. The other is a short brunette, with a cream-colored complexion and a body of a country cowgirl.

The two ladies step inside the house, both carrying shoulder bags and wearing long coats. They stand at the entryway for a moment discussing payment. Once the terms are agreed to, the ladies are directed upstairs to the spare bedroom, where they lay down their things and change into their performance outfits.

Ten minutes later, the ladies descend wearing stilettos and dazzling bikinis. The brunette walks into the center of the living room and asks to turn the music up louder as she starts dancing. The tall stripper walks into the kitchen where Bobby and some of the other guys are gathered around the island countertop.

"I'm Raven — who's the lucky guy?"

Anthony grins and holds his hand above Bobby's head, "This cat right here!"

Raven blows a kiss, "Okay handsome, we have a special dance just for you!"

While Raven is in the kitchen, one of the guys decides to get a little closer to the gal in the living room. She pushes him off and shouts, "Hey, that's not a part of the deal!" then she marches into the kitchen with her partner.

Raven's demeanor changes as she lays out some ground rules, "Fellas, there will be no groping, kissing, or derogatory name calling while we are preforming!"

The guys stand still as if they are being chastised by a grade-school teacher.

She continues, "Anything more than dances will have to be mutually agreed on before moving forward."

One of the guys in the back shouts, "Where did y'all get these stuffy hoes from?!"

Another guy chimes in, "Yeah, I can see this ain't going to be fun already!"

The short brunette snaps back, "I wouldn't talk, as ugly as you are!"

Quickly, profanity is exchanged, and things go south from there.

Anthony makes an executive decision as the owner of the condo. He politely asks the ladies to leave and gives them $200 for their time.

As the girls are gathering their stuff and heading towards the door, one of the guys says, "I wouldn't have given those hoes a single dime!"

The short girl turns and sticks out her middle finger as they walk out the front door. Raven laughs to herself and whispers to her business partner, *"Good job girl — two hundred dollars — and we didn't have to do shit!"*

Back in the condo one of the guys says he has an idea. He asks to use a laptop, places it on the kitchen counter and opens Craigslist. He starts browsing a group called *'Casual Encounters'* while the others gather around.

He lets out a mischievous laugh, "We can find some raunchy broads here that will do anything!"

The guys gather around the computer. One of the guys shouts, "Stop, that's her!! Her name is *'Ginger'* — she's a freak — shoot her a message!"

Within minutes Ginger responds online. After a brief text dialog and exchanging numbers Ginger calls on the phone. She says it would take her forty-five-minutes to get to the bachelor party — and for the right money she will do *anything*.

During the wait the guys continue to drink and joke around. Anthony asks Bobby if he's having a good time. Bobby looks up from his phone and laughs, "Yeah, y'all are funny — I'm having fun just observing you guys."

Anthony smiles, "As long as you're doing good bro, that's all that counts!"

Later the doorbell rings. Anthony rushes over to open it. Ginger walks in holding her head high. She is a good-looking redbone with a voluptuous body and a big afro. She looks around the room to gauge how many men there are. Then she asks for $100 upfront and directions to a restroom so she can get ready. Anthony directs her to the guest bathroom just down the hallway.

While Ginger is in the bathroom getting ready one of the guys shouts, "Now that's what I'm talking about — she's thicker than a snicker!"

All the guys laugh and toss back a few more drinks to prepare for the show.

Five minutes later, Ginger comes out wearing a red, string bikini that is hardly covering anything. She asks to turn the music up loud. She strolls over to the middle of the living room, turns her back to the guys and bends over and grabs her ankles. Immediately guys start cheering and tossing money at her.

While Bobby stays back in the kitchen, Ginger works her way around the room one guy at a time — making sure each one gets a piece of her attention. She whispers a personalized message in each guy's ear.

After brushing up against most of them except for Bobby, Ginger walks into the kitchen to introduce herself to the groom to be, "Hi good looking, do you have any special requests?"

Bobby smiles, "Nah, I'm good — I'm just happy to see my boys having fun. I have a beautiful woman at home that gives me everything that I need."

Ginger replies, "I can respect that!" and gives Bobby a wink of approval.

Ginger turns and makes her way back to the living room full of eager men. This time she gets down on the plush carpet. Now on her hands and knees she arches her back revealing the fullness of her round ass. With a sexy crawl, she makes it to the center of the room. With a snake like slither, she twists her way to the floor and stretches out on her back. She lifts her thick, curvy legs and points her toes to the ceiling. With the smoothness of a ballet dancer, she spreads her legs apart until she is doing a full split.

One of the guys, Eddy, kneels to the floor and starts crawling towards Ginger like a dog in heat. She looks him in the eyes and rubs her thumb across her fingers, signaling that it will cost money to get any closer. Eddy quickly reaches in his pants pocket and clenches a bundle of dollar bills and slaps it on the floor beside her. Ginger glances at the cash, then gives him the go-a-head. He presses his face against the crotch of her red thong panties. He takes a deep sniff and wiggles his head side to side. The other guys break out in cheers and loud laughter.

Then one of the guys goes to the kitchen and grabs a can of spray whip cream from the refrigerator door. He scurries back to the living room and kneels to the carpet. As if she read his mind, Ginger pulls loose the string on her bikini top letting her large breasts fall out. Her dark brown nipples are fully erect. As she lays on her back having her breast covered in whip cream, Eddy is between her legs slowly pulling her panties down over her ankles. He lifts the panties to his face and takes a deep breath before shoving them in the same pocket that once held dollar bills.

Ginger lays on her back completely naked as one guy covers her nipples and naval with the whip cream. Eddy reaches out for the can and sprays a thick line of cream from her clit to her anus. Dollar bills are flying from everywhere as the guys loudly cheer on the freak show.

As the one guy slowly sucks her nipples, Eddy laps up every bit of cream from between her legs. Although Ginger is there to work, she can't help but get extremely turned on by the two men devouring her body with their mouths. The freak show continues. The guys take turns spraying whipped cream and licking it off, until the can is empty.

Ginger gets up from the floor and says she wants to go in the restroom to wash up. She announces that when she returns, she'll be taking special requests as long as the money is right. She asks if there's a private room she can use for the one on one sessions. Anthony points to the guest bedroom at the top of the stairs.

Ginger walks back into the first-floor bathroom and washes up. When she steps out of the restroom, she offers to give the party boy first chance at a private dance. Bobby grins, "I appreciate it, but no thanks, I'm good."

Eddy is the first to take her up on the private one on one sessions. He asks how much it will cost him. She tells him $100 for 15-minutes upstairs. He quickly turns to his buddies, "Somebody give me $100 – I need dat ass! — I'll pay you back!"

Without hesitation Anthony reaches into his wallet and hands his friend a hundred-dollar bill, "Enjoy – it's on me bro!"

Eddy grabs the bill, and like a relay-race runner, he slaps it in Ginger's hand and leads her upstairs. The rest of the guys remain downstairs laughing and throwing back drinks. The night continues.

After a few more guys take turns going upstairs with Ginger, the party starts to wind down. A few of them find places to fall asleep after drinking too much and having sex with the showgirl. One guy lays out on the floor in front of the entertainment system while another guy is stretched out snoring on the couch. It's been a long evening.

Anthony announces, "Whoever wants to stay here for the night, make yourself at home!"

Ginger is upstairs asleep with Eddy. The two of them are cuddled in the guest bed as if they were a couple.

It's now 2:45 am, Bobby is tired and wants to get back to Brianna, but he rode to the party with one of his buddies. He looks around the room trying to gauge who drank the least and would be able to drive him home safely. He asks his friend Derek if he was good enough to drive. Derek says, "Sure, we'll take the back roads to avoid police."

After seeing everybody off, Bobby and Derek get in the car and make their way toward Bobby's house — being careful to take side roads to avoid possible DUI patrols. On the drive Bobby calls Brianna to let her know he's on his way. She tells him that she'll see him when he gets home and to be safe. They hang up the phone.

Suddenly! There is a jolting CRASH! Their car flips upside down shattering every window. The sound of screeching metal echoes in the night as the car spins on the pavement until slamming against a telephone pole. When the car stops moving, Derek is able to crawl out from under the vehicle. He tries to pull Bobby out, but the groom-to-be is unconscious and trapped between his seat and the crushed top of the car. Derek desperately searches for his phone but can't find it in the rubble.

Derek looks up and sees a pickup truck sitting in the middle of the intersection with its hood up and grill ripped off. An intoxicated woman slowly steps out of the vehicle and stumbles over to Derek's car while calling 9-1-1. In an incoherent panic she has trouble describing the accident location. Derek reaches up and grabs her phone to give the operator the exact intersection. He tosses the phone back to the lady and kneels back down next to Bobby, "Hang in there bro! – Help is on the way!"

The fire department and paramedics quickly arrive on scene. Bobby is cut from the vehicle and rushed to the hospital.

Derek finds his phone and shoots a text to all the guys back at the bachelor party, *{Bobby and I were in a car accident. Bobby's unconscious. The ambulance is taking Bobby to Harborview Hospital Emergency room. Meet us there!!}*

Anthony sees the text first and wakes up all the guys. Anthony also calls Bobby's brother Mark to tell him what happened. Mark jumps in his truck and calls Brianna from the drive over. Mark tells her to stay put — he is almost there. He will pick her up and they can ride together.

Brianna freaks out and yells, "I can't wait for you to get here, I have to go now!"

Mark says, "Please wait for me to get there — I'll be there in 5-minutes! He's in safe hands, he's at the best hospital in the country."

Mark pulls up to the house and Bri jumps in. Twenty-minutes later they arrive at the hospital and park in the area reserved for emergency room visitors. They rush inside. Immediately they see the fellas from the bachelor party along with Ginger standing against the wall just outside the emergency room.

Brianna shouts, "WHERE IS BOBBY?!"

Derek steps forward while holding an ice-pack on his wrist, "The staff is prepping him for a CT scan. He's going to be okay!"

"WHERE! I need to see him now!"

Derek points, "Right through that opening — behind the blue curtains to the left!"

Brianna rushes through the doorway with Mark right behind her. She yanks back the heavy drapes, "Baby I'm here!"

Bobby is laying in a gurney with a hospital attendant on each side of him. With puffy eyes and swollen lip, he glances up and grunts, "I'm okay babe..."

At that moment one of the medical staff announces, "Excuse us please, we need to get the patient to the medical imaging room."

As they wheel him away, Mark stands next to Brianna and places his arm around her shoulder, "He's gonna be okay — trust me, my brother is tough."

Ch. 13 - Dollars

After the CT scan and confirmation that Bobby's vitals are stable, he's transported to a standard hospital room for the rest of the night. It's now 4:45 am and he's exhausted from everything that has happened and falls fast asleep. Brianna and Mark tell everyone they can go home for now. The two of them will spend the rest of the night at the hospital with Bobby and will make sure to update everyone in the morning.

While Brianna settles into a chair next to Bobby's bed, Mark steps into the hallway to update his parents and the rest of the family. In a panic, Bobby's mom wants to drop everything and rush to the hospital to be by her son's side, but Mark tells her that Bobby is fine, and his doctors insist that he rest now. Mark assures his mother that Brianna and he will stay right next to Bobby until he's ready for visitors. Reluctantly his mom agrees.

At 8:30 am, Bobby opens his eyes and lets out a moan. Brianna quickly jumps up and leans over him.

"Babe, how do you feel? – Are you in any pain?"

"Naw — I feel pretty numb," still in a daze he looks around the room and continues, "All I remember is — we were driving — and next thing I know I was in an ambulance staring up at a bright light. I vaguely remember a female paramedic looking down at me and saying I was in a rollover car accident."

"Yes, a drunk woman ran a stop sign and T-boned Derek's car on your side — but you are going to be okay baby!"

Just then one of the resident doctors enters the room — Mark quickly follows in behind her.

She is in her thirties, short blond hair, and holding a clipboard full of charts and paperwork. The doctor asks Brianna and Mark to have a seat while she goes over the scan results.

"I'm going to get straight to it," the doctor blurts out, "sir, your lower spine is twisted from the accident. Unless we perform surgery immediately and release the pressure from your spinal cord, you might end up paralyzed for life."

Brianna covers her mouth to keep from screaming. Mark puts his arm around her while looking down at his brother. Bobby just looks away towards the window and doesn't say a word.

The doctor provides more information including what steps have to be taken next and briefly goes over the projected costs.

Because this is a rare procedure that was only recently developed, insurance companies will only cover the hospital stay and physical therapy after the surgery. The surgery itself is going to cost about $400,000 out of pocket. After the doctor provides all the information, she adds that they will need to make a decision within the next 48-hours before scar tissue starts to form around the spine. The doctor finishes by asking if they have any questions.

Without hesitation Brianna responds, "Schedule the surgery now!"

The doctor says, "Okay" and walks out of the room.

Bobby speaks up, "Bri, we don't have four-hundred-thousand dollars. Besides, she said I, *'might be paralyzed,'* that means there's a chance that I won't be..."

Brianna cuts Bobby off, "We can't take that kind of chance babe!" she sniffles and continues, "if there's a procedure that can fix this, we gotta do it! We'll get the money!"

Mark adds, "Yes, we will make it happen!"

***

It's now Saturday afternoon. After Bobby has something to eat, a nurse comes around to check his vitals again. Everything still looks good.

Mark tells Bobby and Bri that he's going to go to his parents' house to brief the family in person — and come back later that evening. Brianna says she will stay there with Bobby and wait for Mark's return. Once Bobby drifts off to sleep from the pain medication, Brianna leaves the room looking for a private area to make a phone call. She opens an emergency exit door and steps into the concrete stairwell. She pulls up her contacts and calls one of her childhood friends from LA.

After two rings the phone picks up.

"Carlos, this is Bri!"

"Hey Chica, it's been a while, how's it going?"

"Not good, I need your help — I need $400,000 for a surgery or my man could be paralyzed for life!"

"Daaamn sis, are you fucken serious?"

"Yes! I'm completely serious — and I'm desperate! Can you please help me?"

"You know I will sis! I got your back always — where are you, so we can talk in person?"

"I'm in Seattle, but I can be there tomorrow morning. I will call you when I'm in town."

"Word! See you soon Chica! Be safe!"

Brianna goes back into the hospital room and stays by Bobby side until Mark returns.

When Mark comes back from his parents' house, Brianna quickly stops him at the hospital room door and takes him back into the hallway. Without going into details, she tells Mark that she's going back to LA to get some help with getting the money. She asks Mark not to tell Bobby about her plans. She wants Mark to stay by Bobby's side and comfort him for the next few days. She plans to stay in constant contact and will be back before the day of the surgery.

Ever since Mark first met Bri, he knew that she was a strong, levelheaded woman, therefore he doesn't question her. She gives Mark a hug and goes back into the hospital room to kiss Bobby and tells him that she loves him. Bobby is drifting in and out of sleep — he is cloudy headed from the pain medications being fed through his IV.

Without going home to pack any clothing, Brianna schedules a ride to the airport using an app on her phone. Within five-minutes she receives a notification that the driver has arrived. She rushes out of the hospital and settles into the back seat.

She arrives at the airport at 7:05 pm, goes straight to the airline counter and purchases a ticket for the next flight to LA which is at 7:55 pm. With little time to spare she rushes through TSA check-in and boarding to catch her flight. The total flight plus runway time only takes about three and a half hours — she expects to be on the ground in LA by no later than 11:30 pm. Once in the air, she realizes she hasn't contacted Carlos since she was at the hospital.

As soon as she lands in Los Angeles, she calls Mark first to give him an update. Mark is in the hospital room watching TV while Bobby is asleep. Her next call is to Carlos.

Carlos answers on the first ring, "Sup Chica!"

Bri shouts, "I'm at the airport, come get me!"

"Damn wonder woman! You got here fast as fuck! Here I come!"

Within thirty-minutes Carlos pulls up to the airport passenger pick-up zone driving his money-green Chevy Impala lowrider. Immediately Brianna recognized him from a distance.

Carlos is slim, with a buzz cut hairdo and a well-trimmed goatee. Along with his finely-detailed tattoos of *Latinas* and *Lowriders* covering both arms — he also has a *LA Lakers* logo tattooed on his left cheekbone and a set of Catholic *Praying Hands* tattooed on the side of his neck. Wearing his signature sunglasses and white tank top, he leans over to the passenger seat and looks up at Brianna, "Damn Chica, I haven't seen you in hella homie! Get in!" Carlos stares at Brianna as she slides into the car. He continues, "You hungry? Let's go get something to eat and talk about a plan to get you that money you need."

They pull up to a 24-hour diner and ask for a booth in the back of the restaurant. They order food but Brianna doesn't touch hers. Between bites Carlos asks Bri how far she's willing to go in order to get the money, and how soon she needs it.

She tells him she will do whatever it takes, as long as no one gets killed in the process. She tells Carlos she needs the money as soon as possible. She explains that the hospital will accept a financial responsibility contract for now, but they will need a letter of assets from a bank to prove the money can be paid before they get started. Because she and Bobby just bought their house, there's no home equity in it yet. She wants to get the money to the hospital, so that there isn't any risk of the doctors refusing to do the surgery.

Carlos listens closely, then says, "Well, I got this idea that I've been planning for years, but I don't trust nobody in this world to share it with — except for you, Chica."

"I know what you mean bro. You and I have been through a lot growing up. I trust you with my life. That's why you were the first person I thought of."

Carlos chuckles, "Yep, remember when my dad used to beat the shit out of me, and you convinced your mom to let me live with you guys? I believe you saved my life. That drunk bastard was going to kill me!"

"Yeah, and I remember you setting that gang member's lowrider on fire in the alley after he grabbed my ass at that house party."

They both laugh as she relaxes and takes her first bite of food.

Carlos says, "Ha – fuck that dude. His ride wasn't shit anyway! Who in the fuck low-rides a fucken Ford?" Carlos laughs so hard that food flies out of his mouth.

"You're so stupid boy!"

After a few more minutes of eating and catching up, Carlos wipes his mouth and goatee. "So, my lil Chica, for years I've been mapping out the perfect plan for bumping-off a money truck. Nobody gets hurt, but I walk away with lots of cash. But I can't do it by myself and I don't trust nobody." Carlos looks around the diner, lowers his voice and continues, "I've gone over my plan a million times in my head and I know it will work. At this point I don't even want the money. I obsess over this plan every day. You, calling me, is a sign. It's time to do it. Now my plan has purpose."

She stares into Carlos's eyes while questions run through her head. Then she blurts out, "Let's do it!"

"Okay, here is the short version. Then we can head back to my place and get some sleep."

Carlos gives a brief description of his plan, "My idea is to stake out large retail stores in the hood. Wait till the money truck comes to pick up the cash to be taken to the bank for deposit. We wait until the money truck completes its last pick-up on its route. By carjacking the truck right before it goes in route to the bank, it will have the most amount of cash on board."

Carlos adds that he has already done the staking out part of the plan and knows what truck will have the most money. He even knows where he wants the heist to happen. All he needs is a second person to pull up in the getaway car.

"Your plan sounds simple enough — how soon can we do it?"

"Slow down Chica! — There's a lot more to it. We'll go over the details tomorrow. I will call my job and tell them that I need to take the next couple days off."

Carlos works in East LA at an auto body shop. He rents out a basement apartment from an older Chicano church lady a few blocks from his job. The lady doesn't drive so Carlos uses her driveway on the side of the house to park his three cars. Besides his low rider, he also has an old pickup truck and a white delivery van.

They finish their food, pay the bill, and drive back to Carlos's apartment. When they pull up at his place, he hands her the keys to the truck and says, "Let's move these two vehicles out so I can get my lowrider tucked away in the back where it's safe for the night."

After the truck and van are out of the way Carlos pulls his lowrider up to the old shed on the side of the house. He detaches his custom steering wheel, opens the hood and removes the distributor cap wire, then he puts a car cover over it and sets the alarm."

Brianna laughs, "This is the part of LA I don't miss! — We don't worry about people taking our cars up in Seattle. A simple alarm does the job there."

Carlos laughs, "Oh hell no, my alarm could be going off for hours and nobody would say shit!"

After playing musical chairs with the vehicles, Carlos takes Brianna into his basement apartment through a side door next to his low rider.

Once inside, Brianna looks around, "Dang bro, you haven't changed a bit!"

All of the walls of the apartment are covered with posters of lowriders and Latina bikini babes. It's a small studio apartment with a cute kitchen, low ceiling, and a queen size futon against the back wall.

"Chica, the bathroom is right there if you need to use it, please excuse the mess."

"It's all good bro! We're family! I don't care about..." she pauses, "Oh shit! I didn't bring any clothes!"

Carlos points to the corner of the room, "Chica, go open that big plastic storage container.

You'll see a fresh pack of boxers and a pack of white wife beaters," he grins and continues, "I save them in case I have a chick over and I'm gonna get some punany!"

They both laugh as Brianna grabs the stuff and goes into the bathroom to take a shower and change. By the time she finishes, Carlos has the futon folded out and has separate covers for himself so that he can lay on top of the spread.

Bri grins, "You've always been a gentleman bro!"

"Shut the fuck up Chica and let's go to sleep."

She laughs and says, "What, Mr. Macho doesn't like being called a gentleman?"

They both laugh and lay down.

Carlos has the TV playing as he's flipping through channels like he does every night before he goes to sleep. Then he hears Brianna sniffling. He looks over — she's crying.

"Chica, it will be all right. Your man will be fine!"

"I'm scared to death," she sniffles and continues, "he is my everything. I couldn't live without Bobby. He has given my life a purpose it never had before."

Carlos leans over and puts his hand on her shoulder, "It'll be okay Chica."

Brianna looks into Carlos's eyes, "Please hold me, I'm scared — I need to be held right now."

With an uncomfortable nervousness, Carlos climbs under the covers. He puts his arms around her from behind making sure not to press up against her body. The two of them fall asleep.

Ch. 14 - Streets of LA

It's Sunday morning. Carlos wakes up at the break of dawn. He is embarrassed and hopes Brianna doesn't notice he woke up with an erection. He quietly climbs out of bed before she notices. Before walking to the bathroom, he looks over and sees Bri is still fast asleep. He steps in the tiny restroom and slowly closes the door — trying not to wake her. After a few private minutes to himself, he jumps in the shower.

When he comes out of the bathroom, Brianna is already in the tiny kitchen making breakfast and coffee, "I found enough stuff to make omelets, is that cool?"

"Hell yeah Chica! – that sounds bomb!"

While Brianna quickly slaps together breakfast, Carlos sits at a small, square kitchen table that looks like it was picked up at a thrift store.

He explains his money truck plan in greater detail, "There's no need for us to follow the money truck for the entire route. We don't want to be spotted. All we have to do is wait at the point of the heist," his voice gets intense as he continues, "I have done a shit-load of research. Two guys always man the truck. A Black dude named Keith and a Latino dude named Junior. Both of these dudes are LA natives and make a basic wage. They drive this route three days a week — Monday, Wednesday, and Friday. The Monday pick up has the most cash. It has all the money from Friday evening to Monday afternoon."

While Carlos goes over his plan, Brianna finishes cooking and serves up two plates before sitting down with him to eat.

He continues, "The first pick up on the route is a Super Walmart. Then the truck picks up money from six large grocery stores in the area. The last stop is about 4:30 in the afternoon at a small convenience store named Jerry's on the edge of town — located in the industrial district. Its customer base is normally factory workers. But since the large lumberyard closed down two years ago, it's been like a ghost town in the area."

Between bites she observes the passion in his face, "Wow, you have really thought this out, haven't you?"

"Hell yeah! To the very last detail!" Carlos stands up before finishing his food and starts pacing around the small apartment, "Jerry's doesn't get a lot of customer traffic in the late afternoon. My plan is to disable the armored truck and enter it as the armed guard goes through the back door from his last pickup. The armored truck always parks on the side of the building, by a green dumpster out of the front view of the little convenience store."

In amazement she asks, "How do you know all of this stuff about disabling an armored truck?"

"Well — a few years ago one of the armored trucks got in a fender bender going through an intersection. Because the armored truck fleet garage is only a few blocks from the body shop I work at, the fleet manager stopped in and asked if we could do some quick bodywork on the shell of the armored truck. The damage was minor, it just needed body filler and paint touch up. It was a special job that my boss asked me to take care of."

Brianna takes one last bite, takes a sip of coffee, and pushes her plate to the side to give Carlos her full attention.

He continues, "But because the paint had to match the company colors exactly, it took a day for the paint to ship and another two days to do the work. I worked on the armored truck over the weekend by myself. In the time that the armored truck sat in the body shop, I completely went through it with a fine, tooth comb."

Brianna can feel the excitement in his voice as he paces back-and-forth, from one corner of the room to the other.

"I have played the scenario in my head a million times. Even though armored trucks have bulletproof glass, foam filled tires, reinforced panel walls, and a metal shield covering the entire underbody — there is a weak point!" Carlos sits down at the table and lowers his voice, *"Behind the inside of both front tires is an opening large enough for the front suspension and reinforced brake lines to move freely when the wheels turn. This design flaw creates a hole big enough to fit a large pair of wire cutters through it."*

Brianna thinks to herself; *this is how Carlos used to get as a kid when he would build model cars and planes. He would get so intense and treat the toys as if they were real.*

Carlos uses his index finger to make an invisible drawing on the tabletop, "Just inside the right-side opening is a 4-gauge power cable that runs from the primary battery to the vehicle's starter motor. If this wire is cut, the armored truck will not start again once the engine is turned off. Even though they'll still have cell phones and can call for backup, the response time will be 12 to 15-minutes due to LA traffic and it being on the outskirts of town."

Carlos gets up from the table again, and reaches up into one of the kitchen cabinets and pulls out a blue folder full of printed photos and tosses them on the table, "The heist should take no longer than 6-minutes to get all of the money unloaded and into the getaway car."

Brianna sifts through the photos, "You have photos of the armor truck?"

"Yeah Chica, I took lots of them with my cell phone while the truck was in my shop."

"So how are you going to get under the truck to cut this wire?'

Carlos laughs, "I'm going to be laying against the side of the building by the green dumpster, with a dirty blanket covering me. When the armored truck pulls up, they'll never notice me. People never pay attention to homeless people. Once the truck is parked, I'll roll underneath it, quickly cut the cable and roll back out."

"It's that easy huh?"

"Yeah — it's that easy Chica!" Carlos continues laying out his plan while sorting the photos and his notes. He has pictures of both the inside, and the outside of the armored truck. He continues to lay out his plan, "There are two ways to lock and unlock the back of the armored truck. One is a switch on the dashboard that the driver controls. The other is a large keyhole on the rear door. The key is cuffed to the wrist of the guard making the pickups. As sophisticated as it seems, it's also a very basic system that has been in place for many years."

She asks, "So which guard is going to open the rear door for us?"

"The pick-up guard! When he comes out of Jerry's mini-mart, I'm going to be right there!"

"Will you have a gun?" Brianna's eyes open wide.

"Yes, but I'm not going to shoot anyone."

"The guards have guns too, right?" she asks.

"Yep, but we will make sure they don't think about pulling them out!"

"How are WE going to do that?"

Carlos laughs, "With dynamite and a ransom note!"

Carlos gets up from the table and puts his plate in the sink while Brianna stares at the back of his head like he's crazy. Carlos gives more details while walking around the small apartment.

"We will print and slap a stick-up note on the windshield of the armored truck for the driver to read. The note will say, [*We know who you are and where you live. Do not try anything!]*"

"Okay — go on," she says.

"We will create a device to look like a bomb out of road flares, wires, and a digital timer. There's a photograph of the prototype at the bottom of that stack of pictures. I found the design on a website for creating movie props."

Bri asks, "So, I get what the note is for, but what about this fake bomb?"

"When we slap the note on the windshield of the armored truck we're going to quickly show the driver the fake bomb and then toss it underneath the truck. It's just another form of intimidation so that the driver doesn't try to call for backup."

Brianna's head is swirling with thoughts as she worries about this plan Carlos is laying out. Right then Carlos sits down on the small loveseat and fires up a joint. "You want to hit this weed Chica?" he says.

"Naw — I'm good. I'm going to step outside to call and check on Bobby."

"Cool – after you're done on the phone let's drive across town to Jerry's mini-mart so I can show you where it's all gonna go down."

"Okay!"

Then Bri steps out into the driveway on the side of the house. Leaning against Carlos's lowrider she calls Mark, "Hi, how's Bobby doing this morning?"

"Hey sis, he's good. He's sleeping again. The pain medicine he's on has him out like a log. How's it going with you — are you okay?"

"I'm good. I'm still working on getting the money. Are you next to Bobby?"

"I was — but I'm stepping out in the hallway right now so we can talk without waking him," Mark continues, "A few things to report — Bobby has a spinal cord injury specialist coming up to the hospital tomorrow morning. Bobby insisted on getting a second opinion before scheduling the surgery. You know how my brother is."

Brianna sniffles, "I think that's a great idea — I should have thought of that myself before taking off."

Mark goes on, "The specialist is going to examine the CT scan and run a few body muscle response tests on Bobby. They should be able to give us their opinion immediately."

"Mark — please call me as soon as you get the results — please!"

"I will. Is everything else okay?"

"Yeah — can you wake up Bobby for a second? I need to hear his voice."

"Yep — hold on while I walk back into the room."

Mark puts his phone to Bobby's ear, "Wake up bro, it's Bri, she wants to talk to you."

Bobby is groggy but coherent, "Babe — where are you, and what are you doing?"

"I'm in LA — trying to get the money for your surgery."

"You got to be fucking kidding me!" Bobby coughs and goes on, "Get back home! We are a team! We don't go off and do things like that by ourselves. I need you by my side right now!"

There's a brief moment of silence before Brianna starts crying. "You're right Bobby! I don't know what I was thinking!" Through her sniffles she pushes out, "I'm so sorry babe. I will be back as quick as I can."

"Be safe babe – I'll see you soon – I love you!"

"I love you too!"

Brianna walks back into the apartment.

Carlos can tell she's been crying, "Is everything okay Chica? How's your man doing?"

"He has a spinal cord specialist coming to see him today. Bobby wants to get a second opinion before scheduling the surgery."

"That makes hella sense Chica!"

Brianna stands in the middle of the room for a moment thinking before she speaks, "I'm going to take a shower."

In the bathroom she just stares at her bloodshot eyes in the mirror and thinks to herself, *'What the fuck am I doing here?'*

After a long hot shower and getting dressed she steps out and looks around for Carlos. He is outside shifting his vehicles around so he can get his lowrider ready to drive.

A few more minutes go by before he steps back into the apartment, "Hey Chica, it was a fun fantasy while it lasted wasn't it?" and starts laughing.

"Yeah — it was," she takes a look around the apartment as if it will be her last time seeing it. "Carlos, can you take me to the airport now?"

"You got it sis! The car is already pulled out and ready for you."

On the drive to the airport, Brianna looks over at Carlos, "Can you drive past Jerry's mini-mart? You have me curious and I want to see what it looks like."

Carlos pushes his sunglasses up on his nose and grins, "Sure thang!" then makes a quick left-hand turn — spinning his tires and tossing up a cloud of dust.

When they pull up to the convenience store it's vacant. A sign on the glass door reads, *Closed On Sundays*. The two of them get out of the car and lean against it, daydreaming about the heist that almost happened. A few minutes go by without a word spoken — each contemplating their own thoughts.

After five-minutes pass, Carlos turns to Brianna, "Come on Chica, if we want to get you a flight to Seattle tonight, we gotta go now."

Ch. 15 - Painkillers

Brianna's flight arrives in Seattle at 6:30 Sunday evening. She quickly hails the first taxi she sees. When she gets back to the hospital, Bobby's room is filled with people. His mom and dad, his sister, cousins, aunts, uncles, his friends from the bachelor party, and Mark are all there.

She immediately feels the anxiety she had the first time she met Bobby's family at the Thanksgiving gathering. Her shyness overwhelms her as she makes her way through the crowded room. She can hear her name being whispered by different people, but all she can do is concentrate on making it to Bobby.

Folks step to the side to let her through. She stops at Bobby's bedside and starts crying. Bobby reaches up with one arm and tugs at her to lean in close. He kisses her tears, "Baby, I'm going to be okay — I promise."

Brianna turns and scans the room to see so many people — she can't count them all. Some of the faces she has never seen before. She leans back down and whispers in Bobby's ear, *"I'm never leaving you like that again."*

Now that she's there, the visitors start getting ready to leave. Each person coming over and giving Brianna a hug and giving Bobby their well wishes. His mother and father are the last to leave, but before they do, Bobby's mom takes Brianna by the hands, "Girl, Bobby told me that you went to California to try to borrow the money for his procedure. Don't worry about that, our family has plenty of resources and we have property. We will be able to come up with the money when the time comes. You just stay here and stay by my son's side, let me worry about the money — you hear me sweetie?"

"Yes ma'am! – I should have come to you before leaving — I guess I panicked. I was thinking, if we didn't have the money the doctors wouldn't help my Bobby."

Bobby's mom kisses Brianna on the forehead, "I understand baby girl. You went into survival mode. I get it — I've been there. But as we get older, we learn sometimes, we have to stop and think before taking action."

Brianna wraps her arms around Bobby's mother and hugs her as tight as she can, and whispers, *"Thank you… Mom."*

***

Early the next morning, the spinal cord specialist, Dr. Edward Jackson III, walks in the room just after Bobby finishes breakfast. Only

Brianna and Mark are at the hospital with Bobby this early in the day.

Dr. Jackson is a tall slender Black man in his sixties. He has worked with spinal cord and back injuries his entire career. He graduated at the top of his class at St. George's University, School of Medicine 40-years ago. He was the only African-American student at the time.

In an authoritative voice the doctor begins, "Son, I have reviewed copies of all your medical records, including the CT scans and X-Rays," he goes on to explain, "I will perform a series of tests which include body movement and nerve sensitivity detection. This will take about an hour, so let's get started."

Bobby responds, "Can my brother and fiancé stay in the room?"

"Yes they can. In fact, I prefer they do."

Dr. Jackson tells Brianna and Mark to stand on the other side of the bed so that they can see what he's doing. but still be out of the way. Within minutes, they can see that he is a thorough doctor that cares about his patients.

The doctor goes on to explain each test before he performs it. He uses stainless steel rods that look like chopsticks to probe specific spots on Bobby's spine. Each time he pushes in on a spot, he asks Bobby if he can feel it. Dr. Jackson writes down the results on a clipboard and continues with the next test. He has Bobby do his best to roll from one side to the other — then has Bobby move his toes, ankles, hands, and arms before having Bobby take a series of deep breaths.

As the doctor is performing these tests, Brianna looks across the bed and impatiently asks, "How long before we get the results?"

With a confident smile Dr. Jackson replies, "There's nothing wrong with him. What he has is simple old-fashioned whiplash. It will subside in a couple of weeks. His back muscles are merely locked up around his spine. This is the body's natural way of protecting itself. All this boy needs — is rest."

Brianna can't believe what she's hearing and faints just as Mark catches her.

Bobby shouts, "BABY!!"

Dr. Jackson quickly places his hand on Bobby's chest to keep him from trying to sit up. Then the doctor looks over to Mark, "She'll be okay, just sit her down in that chair — she'll come to."

Mark lowers Brianna into the chair and sits next to her, while patting the back of her hand. Within a few minutes, she slowly opens her eyes. She's a little disorientated. Mark hands her a bottled water and tells her to take a sip.

As Dr. Jackson finishes up with the final tests and questions, Brianna sits quietly staring at Bobby. The doctor fills out a few more things on the clipboard and concludes by saying, "I'm going to prescribe some muscle relaxers and painkillers —

You also need to take time off from work and stay in bed for the next three weeks."

"When can my man come home?" Brianna says with excitement.

Dr. Jackson looks up from the clipboard, "I will start the paperwork for his release as soon as I get back to my office. He should be able to go home by tomorrow morning."

Mark jumps to his feet, "Are you serious?!"

"Yes – I am completely serious. He will be back to normal soon, as long as he does as I say and rests." Dr. Jackson glances over to Brianna, then looks down at Bobby and continues, "This is a common injury. I will be handing you a recovery plan — follow it to the letter and call my office if anything changes or if you have questions. I'll be back in the morning for a final assessment before you are released from the hospital."

Mark can't contain his joy, "Bro, I'm going outside to call Mom and Dad — and the others!"

Bobby gives his brother a smile and looks at Brianna, "Babe, come here – Everything is going to be great from here on out!"

With tears, she leans down, "You promise?"

"Yes, I promise!"

Ch. 16 - Freeway Chase

The last evening at the hospital — Bobby, Brianna, and Mark sit and talk while flipping channels on the hospital room television. Earlier, Mark stepped out to pick up pizza and sodas. While they eat, Mark informs Bobby and Bri that he told everyone about Bobby's prognosis and release from the hospital in the morning. Mark laughs and says their mother was so happy she just kept screaming over the phone, *"God is good! — God is good!"* she wouldn't stop until their dad took the phone from her.

Brianna pulls her chair next to Bobby's bedside while holding his hand tightly. Mark continues flipping channels until he hits CNN.

There is a breaking story out of Los Angeles about a high-speed freeway chase.

Mark laughs, "Check out this fool on TV!"

Brianna looks up at the screen and freezes like she's seen a ghost, "OH GOD — he did it!"

Confused, Bobby asks, "Bri! What are you talking about?!"

Bri replies, "That's my brother Carlos running from the police!"

"I thought you only had *one* brother?"

"He's my hood brother — my pretend brother." Brianna stares at the TV in shock, "He said he wasn't going to do it, but he did anyway!"

With disappointment Bobby glares at Brianna, "Is that what you were in LA for!?"

She drops her head in regret, "Yes babe — I'm so sorry Bobby."

***

The helicopter footage of the car chase is being aired live on the west coast, including at Purdy Women's Correctional Facility where Bobby's ex Trish, is serving time, for attempting to kill Brianna at the old apartment. Trish is sitting at a table in the common area with other female inmates when the story breaks.

One of the females walking past, looks up at the TV and laughs, "Look at this Cholo in LA — running from the police in a fuckin lowrider."

The women at the table, all stop what they're doing and watch the police chase unfold.

***

Bobby, Brianna, and Mark are glued to the TV, not missing a single detail. The news anchor announces, *"There appears to be only one person in the fleeing vehicle."* Then pauses while the helicopter camera zooms in closer. The anchor continues, *"There are early reports that this high-*

speed chase is the result of an attempted armored truck heist."

"OH Fuck!" Mark blurts out.

Bobby is completely speechless as he turns his head back and forth between the TV and Brianna.

***

As the freeway chase continues, Carlos slows his car down and hits his hydraulic switches a few times — front-back, then side-to-side before stopping in the middle lane of the I-5 interstate.

Carlos slams his lowrider to the ground and turns off the engine. He puts both hands out the driver's window, so that the police and the helicopter above can see he is not holding a weapon. He reaches out and opens the car door from the outer handle and slowly steps out. Wearing his work coveralls, he gets down to his knees as if he's been through this routine before. He puts his hands behind his head and looks up at the helicopter news camera with a huge smile before being tackled and taken into custody.

Across the country people are cheering for what appears to be a hard-working man that just wanted a break in life. The public is so used to high-speed chases ending with the suspect being killed before being taken into custody — this ending is a relief to everyone. Even the local news is spinning the story with a *Robin Hood* twist.

For the next hour, the helicopter continues to hover over the scene while news anchors back at the studio release more details.

The news is reporting that the police have parking lot surveillance video from the convenience store showing Carlos and an unidentified woman standing next to the getaway car. Local authorities and the FBI want to bring the unidentified woman in for questioning. Police are asking the public for their assistance in identifying her.

***

Back at Purdy women's prison, Trish blurts out, "I know that little bitch! That's the bitch that put me in here."

One of the other girls at the table says, "Girl, the Feds will give you time off if you help them solve a federal case like this — girl you need to talk to somebody right away — this could be your meal ticket out of here!"

Trish stands up from the table and yells, "GUARD! GUARD! — I need to talk to somebody — right now!!"

Ch. 17 - Orange Jumpsuits

Between the surveillance video footage, Trish's tip to the Feds, and phone call records between Brianna and Carlos, a judge issues an arrest warrant to take Brianna into custody pending a full investigation.

Brianna is picked up and flown to Los Angeles County Jail to be held until her first court date. She is considered a high flight risk due to her trips back-and-forth between Seattle and LA, so the judge denies her bail.

***

Brianna wakes up early her first morning in jail. The individual cell doors are open for the women to go into the common area. There is a single community payphone mounted to a concreate wall with a six-foot long wooden bench just to the right of it. Brianna approaches the bench and sits down in line for her turn to make a call. There is one inmate on the phone and two others waiting before her.

While waiting her turn to use the phone, a masculine looking female with lots of tattoos and long black hair approaches Brianna, "I like your braids." She sits down on the bench beside Bri.

Brianna shrugs and slides away a few inches. The woman smirks and reaches for one of Brianna's braids, "I want you to do my hair just like yours — sweety."

Brianna pulls away, "No thank you!"

"That was not a request little bitch! — I'm TELLING you to braid my hair!"

Other inmates nearby stop what they are doing and watch for what's about to happen next.

With a fierce confidence, the bully gets up from the bench and struts over to the floor mounted table in the middle of the room. At the table, two inmates are sitting talking. The bully bends and swipes her forearm across the table like a windshield wiper blade, knocking dominoes and playing cards off onto the floor. One of the two inmates at the table has a standard-issue black plastic comb wedged in the back of her afro. Without saying a word, the bully snatches the comb then turns back to look at Brianna. Holding the comb like a weapon the bully glares and gestures for Brianna to come over to the table.

Bri pauses for a moment, then slowly gets up from the bench and walks over to the bully. She reluctantly takes the comb, "Okay, let's do this quickly so I can get back to making my phone call."

"Don't rush me little bitch! — Do my shit right!"

"Well sit down then!" Brianna stands behind the bully and looks down at her head, "We have to wet your head a little so this cheap ass comb will go through your thick hair."

The bully motions to another inmate to go get a paper cup full of warm water.

Brianna takes the cup and sits it on the table within reach, "Somebody, hand me a towel so I don't get her shoulders wet."

"Yeah, you better not get me wet little bitch!"

One of the other girls has a bath towel wrapped around her hair after just getting out the community shower, and hands her towel to Brianna.

"Okay, I have everything I need to hook you up. Now lift up the back of your hair and hold it so I can lay this towel over your shoulders."

As soon as she raises the back of her hair, Brianna quickly ropes the towel around the bully's neck. Brianna pulls and twists as tight as she can while wedging her knee in the inmate's spine. Within seconds, the bully's eyes roll to the back of her head. She flops her legs and gasps for air like a fish out of water. Brianna wrenches tighter on the towel while the other women step back in shock. Nobody attempts to break it up.

The bully blacks-out and goes limp. Brianna lowers her to the floor and stands over her body, "BITCH! You stepped to the WRONG one today! Growing up on my block, we crushed *manly* bitches like you for fun!"

The guards finally notice the commotion and rush in to break it up. Brianna is taken into solitary confinement and given an additional assault charge. She is allowed one call to her lawyer or whomever she desires. She calls Bobby and tells him what happened.

Bobby does his best to give words of encouragement, "Don't worry babe, I'm working on getting you the best lawyer in the world! Keep your head up. Babe — we're going to get you out of there soon. Think of it this way — in solitary confinement no one can mess with you again. Stay strong babe! I love you!"

***

A few weeks pass and Brianna starts feeling sick to her stomach each morning. The jail nurse gives her a blood test which reveals that she's pregnant. The news draws uncontrollable tears to Brianna's face. She trembles while thinking of a way to break the news to Bobby.

Because of her pregnancy the Warden decides to keep her in confinement indefinitely for her safety. While in solitary confinement, she is only allowed one phone call a week. To pass time until her next call, she lays in her bunk staring at the ceiling and thinking about her life. It's an extremely lonely and depressing time for her.

Monday morning, after having breakfast served in her small jail cell, a female guard opens the door. Brianna is led down a dimly lit hallway to a payphone attached to a wall. Her entire body shakes as she dials the phone.

Bobby answers on the first ring, "Babe!!"

Brianna sniffles, "I miss you so much Bobby."

"Bri, how are you doing? Are you okay?"

After a long pause Brianna whispers, *"I'm pregnant..."*

Then the phone goes silent on both ends.

Ch. 18 - County Courthouse

Brianna spends a total of eight months in Los Angeles County Jail and multiple appearances in front of the judge before her lawyer was able to prove to the court that she had no control over Carlos's actions — and that he acted alone. Carlos backed up Brianna's lawyer by making a sworn statement that she had nothing to do with his attempted armored truck heist, and the plan was fully his.

Because of Carlos's sworn statement, having no prior convictions, and being pregnant, the judge drops all charges, including the jail assault, and dismisses the case.

Six-weeks before her due date, Brianna is flown back to the Seattle, King County Jail to spend three more days for final processing before being released. If she had spent another two-weeks in jail she would not been allowed to fly and would have had to travel by Greyhound bus with a police escort.

On the day of her freedom, she is given her original clothing and property. Because of her baby-bump, she is unable to fasten her pants, so she ties her jacket around her waist backwards and lets it drape down like an apron.

Bobby waits in the lobby of the jail house as she is led out the last secure door from the building. They are both immediately overwhelmed with emotions. Brianna stops in her tracks and starts shaking as tears pour down her cheeks. Bobby's throat is so tight, he is unable to utter a word. He rushes over to Brianna as if to catch her before she collapses. He awkwardly fumbles, to figure out a way to hold her tight, without pressing against their baby.

When they leave the jail house, Bobby leads Brianna across the street and into the County Courthouse building.

With complete confusion Brianna asks, "Where are we going Bobby?"

"Brianna, when you wake up tomorrow morning, you are going to be a married woman!"

Ch. 19 - Life Continues

Although their lawyer got her out of jail without any charges, it was Trish's tip that helped the federal agents first track Brianna down.

Because of Trish's willingness to help the Feds, she receives time shaved off her sentence. While in prison, Trish begins hanging out with an inmate, that gave her the suggestion to reach out to the Feds. As months pass, Trish's friendship with the inmate turns into an intimate relationship. For the first time in Trish's life, she feels mentally free. She is now able to strip off her hard, exterior image and the materialistic lifestyle that controlled her before. She falls in love with the inmate, and they get married in jail.

***

Fifteen months pass since the failed heist before Brianna is able to talk with Carlos on the phone again. Until now only brief hand-written letters could be exchanged between each other.

To Brianna's surprise, Carlos makes a collect call to her from prison one day.

"Hey Bro! How are you doing?"

"I'm doing great Chica! How is life being a new mom?"

"It's more wonderful than I could have ever imagined. Bobby is the best father in the world to my little ball of happiness. I will mail you pictures of her soon!"

"I can't wait to see her! — I'm so happy for you sis!"

"Carlos, how are you handling the joint?"

"I'm doing great!" he replies, "I'm the *'Lowrider Bandido'* up in this camp!"

Brianna laughs, "What do you mean?"

"Chica — I have something in my life now that I could not have gotten any other way. I'm a *hero* up in this mother fucker — and it feels great!"

Brianna starts to feel sad, "I love you bro!"

"I love you too sis, and one day I'll be out of here. I'll go back to doing bodywork and I'll finish my life having a legacy over my head."

Feeling a bit doubtful she asks, "Are you really okay Carlos?"

"Seriously, I'm good Chica — don't worry about me. I'm in prison with all my homies anyway." Carlos laughs and continues, "The homies got my back — this is going to be easy time. I might do six-years max, if I stay out of trouble. Shit, I won't even be 35-years-old when I get out this mother fucker. I'll have a whole life ahead of me and I'll be known as a hero in the streets! I'm the *Lowrider Bandido*."

They both laugh just as an automated voice suddenly cuts in, *"You have one-minute left for this call."*

"Okay bro, take care of yourself!"

"Wait Chica! One more thing!" Carlos quickly lets out, "This shit haunted me all my life, I would have died wondering if I could pull this off. I swear to god, I know what I did wrong, I almost had it!"

They both laugh again, and end the call knowing that everything was going to be okay.

***

Over the next few months, the car accident case settles. The insurance company for the intoxicated woman who ran the stop sign, paid all of Bobby's medical bills.

Bobby also picked up a high-profile accident lawyer that went in hard and sued for future pain and suffering. The lawyer convinced the jury, that

Brianna's jail time was a direct result of her desperation to help her fiancé after he was hospitalized. The lawyer brought in a psychologist and other experts to show the jury that the possibility of further emotional trauma for Bobby and his family was high. The accident lawyer sued for $8 million, and settled for $4.3 million. The lawyer took $1.5 million which was one-third of the settlement, leaving Bobby and Brianna with the remaining two-thirds — about $2.8 million.

Ch. 20 - Roses

Exactly one year has passed since Brianna's release from jail and their courthouse marriage, and two years since they met in the airport. It's early Saturday morning, the sun is peeking through the blinds. Bri looks around the bedroom, but Bobby and the baby are not there. She walks into the living room full of Red Roses everywhere, "Oh my god babe!"

Bobby steps out of the kitchen, "Happy Anniversary!" He kisses her on the lips and smiles, "I made you a special breakfast, have a seat and enjoy. After I feed you, I have something special planned."

She looks around the room in a panic, "Babe! Where's Angel?"

"My mom stopped by about an hour ago and picked her up for the weekend so we can have this time alone!"

"Wait, what do you mean, the weekend? Is she going to be gone overnight?!"

"Yes babe — overnight. I know we've never let her stay the night away from us, but it's time. She'll be safe with my mom. Relax, I made you a champagne breakfast."

Brianna quickly sits down at the table, "Give me the whole fucken bottle, I'm going to need it!"

They both laugh.

After eating and chugging down a half bottle of champagne, Bri feels relaxed and a little frisky.

"Bobby, let's take a shower together!"

"Girl, you don't have to ask me twice!"

Brianna puts back one more swallow of champagne before the two of them scrimmage to the bathroom. They strip and get under the hot water. There is a moment of déjà vu, as he pulls her close to him and stares into her chestnut brown eyes.

"Brianna, you are my life, you are my everything. From the first day I laid eyes on you, I wanted to hold you and never let you go."

Brianna backs herself into the corner of the shower and lifts one leg onto the edge of the tub and pulls Bobby to her. He kisses her on the lips before slowly kneeling and kissing down the middle of her stomach until he stops between her legs. She places her hand on to the back of his head as he treats himself to the sweetest dessert he can imagine.

Like drinking from a fountain, he presses his mouth over her wet peach as the warm water runs down her stomach and over his lips.

After a few minutes she moans, "Babe, I can't take this any longer, my legs are getting weak — let's go get in the bed."

Bobby stands and steps out the shower and grabs a towel to dry Brianna off. She runs and jumps in the bed while he dries himself.

"Babe come give it to me hard! I need you deep inside of me!"

Bobby stands in the doorway looking at her laying there with her knees up. He climbs up on the bed and gives her sweet-fruit one last lick before slowly sliding into her warm body. She feels his pulse throbbing inside of her as if he is going to explode. They look deep into each other's eyes as their bodies press together.

Brianna starts to tear up as her life with Bobby flashes through her mind. She sniffles and whispers, *"Babe, I'm about to cum…"*

Bobby's eyes get bigger as he pushes in as deep as he can. She lets out a soft squeal, as she feels him enter the deepest parts of her body.

"Babe!" she cries out, "I'm cumming!!"

He looks deep into her eyes, "I love you Brianna!"

"I love you too, Bobby!"

Bobby's eyes roll back as he releases himself. She wraps her legs and arms around him tight. She pulls him as close to her as she can. He collapses on top of her and the two of them lay in each other's arms almost breathless.

After a few minutes of silence, Brianna looks up into Bobby's eyes and *softly* asks, *"Babe — why do you love me so much?"*

Bobby kisses her on the forehead, "Because you are my best friend. We can talk about anything. You have never tried to change me. You've never wanted to have me walk, talk, or dress in a different way. You've never asked me to change my beliefs. You always except me for me, and I appreciate that. I know that you love us, but I also know that you love me even more. I believe you would take a bullet for me."

"Yes babe — I *would* take a bullet for you — I would take a *whole* clip. We are a team — you have my best interests at heart. You look out for my health and my mental well-being. When I am about to make a mistake that could hurt me, you step in and lift me up. You find my strengths and encourage me to be the best I can be. You are my protector, my man, my husband. I will love you forever!"

He smiles, "Happy Anniversary Bri!"
"Happy Anniversary my Bobby!"

The two hold each other as they drift off to sleep — knowing life is good.

The End

…for now, that is.

Coming soon, Book II in this Series;

Diamonds Dollars & Palm Trees

It's the year 2021, Carlos is out on parole but can't stop thinking about the heist that almost succeeded. Trish is released early from Purdy Women's Prison to help stop the spread of COVID-19. If she gets in trouble for anything else she could be sent back to lockdown and required to serve out her entire sentence of 14-years — but she still holds a grudge. Bobby's brother Mark takes on a job as a Seattle police officer. Brianna's biological brother Jimmy moves from LA to Seattle to be closer to his sister and niece. Jimmy is a good person at heart but him and his motorcycle tend to find trouble wherever they're at. Ginger leaves the call-girl business and enrolls in nursing school and is now working in the same hospital that Bobby was rushed to. Plus, the introduction of new colorful characters that promise to entertain. As for Bobby and Brianna, they decide to travel and see the world — and *The Fire Continues…*

(see more on next page…)

Acknowledgments

I want to thank all of the people who inspired and helped me through the process of finishing this book. This book would not be possible without the support of many people.

First and Foremost!
My Business & Writing Partner
Author, Nicole A. Calvo.
No single person has been more encouraging or supportive over the years. This book truly would have never gotten completed without her influence and encouragement. Please pick up her amazing true story,
"The Ragdoll and The Marine"
You won't be disappointed.
Available on Amazon & NicoleCalvo.com

Special Thanks to the Proofreading Team
In Alphabetical Order by First Name:
Kimberly Smith
Kristee Crowder
Linda Smith
Susan McCants
Tinna White

(continued on next page…)

**Thanks to My English Composition
Teacher at Bellevue College!
Dr. Hyesu Park, Ph.D.**
Your class was invaluable and changed the direction of
my writing forever. Receiving an A in your class was
one of my biggest academic achievements in life.

**Thanks to my fellow Authors in the writing
community who live "The Writers Life."**

In Alphabetical Order by First Name:

Author, April Craft
Author, David Beachem
Author, Edward Ezell
Author, Helen Collier
Author, Jeffrey L. Cheatham II
Author, Lee Yusuf
Author, Mohamed Awaleh
Author, Robert "Bob" Bly
Author, Shanteria Tipler
Author, Sharonda Webb
Author, Terry Hill
Author, Troy Landrum, Jr.
Author, Vee Cormier
- and -
Author, Donald Goines (RIP)
*The amazing story teller that inspired me at age 15 to
want to write a book one day.*

(continued on next page…)

Honorable Mentions

Author & Book Publisher, Sharon Blake
Life Chronicles Publishing LLC
Thanks for sending all those editing, and consulting jobs my way over the years. We have worked on some wonderful projects together and hopefully there will be many more to come!

Author, Alvin L.A. Horn
I'm proud to call this veteran writer my friend, as well as my mentor. I have the utmost respect for a man that can drop words onto pages as eloquently as a flowing river. I aspire to one-day write at the level of this literary genius. If you haven't read his work yet, please do!
AlvinHorn.com

Chief Editor, Dennis Beaver
The Northwest Facts Newspaper - nwfacts.com
Thanks for publishing my articles on "*Diversity in The Workplace*" in your newspaper over the last few years. I look forward to continuing our journalism work together.

(continued on next page…)

Additional Acknowledgments & Inspirational People

My Father, General C. Huguley
Thanks for introducing me to photography as a kid, and for making a big deal of all of my drawings, comic strips, and corny childhood artwork!
You Are My Biggest Inspiration!

My brother, Raquib Mu'ied (aka Gregory Huguley)
My multi-talented nephew, Elijah Mu'ied
And the rest of my very talented Huguley bloodline!

Singer/Song Writer, Richard "Daddy Rich" Lowery
"Sir-Mix-A-Lot" Anthony L. Ray
"Nasty" Nes Rodriguez

Seattle Magic Wheels MC
Emerald City Fish & Chips
Seattle VA Hospital Staff
Lidline Sports with Granville Emerson
Seattle's Own, Rainier Avenue Radio
Ezell Stephens, owner & founder of,
"Heaven Sent Fried Chicken"

And Lastly…

Thanks to all the *"Haters"* & *"Stockers"*
that are reading this right now!!
lmao ☺

Book Fun Facts

The original book title was, Memories Before Midnight.

I wrote 75% of the book in one week, in November 2018.

From November 2018 until 5/21/20 Brianna's original name was Monika. I changed it during editing.

Robert "Bobby" King's name is a combination of Bobby Seale & Martin Luther King.

The call girl named Raven was originally named Cherish.

I designed and created my book cover after a graphic designer in Russia ripped me off for my deposit through PayPal on May 16th, 2020 — then ghosted me. So, although he kept my money and never delivered anything, the cover design I created is better than anything he could have ever produced! Things work out for a reason.
#winner ☺

Hold your phone's camera over this QR Code

to view samples of my photography

From the Author

Thank you for purchasing my book! If you enjoyed it, please write a review on **Amazon,** and share the title with someone you know. By doing so, you'll help me to produce more work. Book II of this series is in production and will be released as soon as possible. I have other titles that I'm working on as well, stay tuned!

I would love to hear your feedback. Please text or email me at: **(425) 624-5368**, or **mrhuguley@msn.com**. I will personally read every message. You can also leave a voice mail.

To receive **FREE** promotional giveaways, book discounts, and updates about future title releases, please shoot me a *text* or *email* with the words, "SIGN ME UP."

If you have a story that you would like to write or a project you need edited, please visit my website *www.johnhuguley.com*. Let me help you take the next step towards getting published.

~ John A. Huguley
Author | Editor | Freelance Journalist

Final Thought

"You should never have to work hard to hold on to a good partner;
When you're good to them, they will be busy holding on to you…"

~ J. A. Huguley